THE INNOVATORS

BOOK 1 – LEAVING DREAMLAND

BY GREG GILLIS-SMITH

ALPIN PRESS

CALIFORNIA

For Paul and Elyse.

And Dedicated to all the nerds in this world

Thanks to my wonderful wife,

who always believes in me

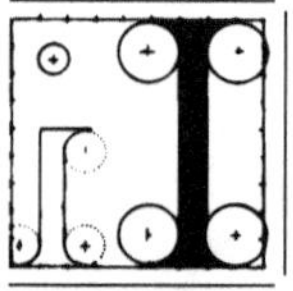

INTRODUCTION

I love reading adventure stories, but I am often left wanting more as I strive to duplicate the 'magic' we read and see on screen. Try as we might we cannot recite the spell and levitate our younger sibling out of the room. I have written this book to allow the reader to do the engineering, use the concepts to innovate their own inventions and fly by the calculations of their own mind. You can literally build and duplicate everything in this book on your own. I don't, however, recommend trying to get a vehicle to float on a raft.

The QR codes point to a link or video to see more detail. Use an app like QR Code Reader to follow the link. Speaking of detail, you can read my blog on gillis-smithauthor.com to see some of my research process.

If you want to connect with Mr. Alpin, see the Facebook page, www.facebook.com/groups/TheInnovatorsBooks. Younger readers can just enjoy the story while older readers can expand on the concept and build their own. By the way, yes, most books spell numbers less than 10, but this book uses a numeral for any number that is mathematical. Enjoy and always be innovating.

"Innovation distinguishes between a leader and a follower."
- *Steve Jobs*

CHAPTER 1 – NEW FACES

If you look at history, innovation doesn't come just from giving people incentives; it comes from creating environments where their ideas can connect. - Steven Johnson

Tap-tap-tap. Clunk. Tap. Tap-tap-tap-tap.[i] The pen nervously tapped at the edge of the old worktable. The late morning light streamed across the lab, but eyes were still half shut against the glare. The scent of fresh floor polish and pine-scented cleaner was mixed with the usual smells of cutting fluid, lumber, and other supplies. Students shifted awkwardly in their seats and whispered to one another. They all had one thing in common, no one knew their new teacher, not even his or her name. This was not a typical group of kids; they were engineering students at Hundred Oaks Polytechnic Experience.

The door opened to the windless oppressive heat that is only punctuated by the seemingly unexpected thunderstorms that happen every August. The dry Santa Ana winds don't usually start for another month or two, making the beginning of school synonymous with one's legs sticking to beige plastic chairs.

The students, mostly juniors and seniors, had been together for several years in various science and math classes. Their previous teacher had moved away over the summer, and they wondered what their year would be like. They were not the popular ones, not to say that they are unpopular, they are sometimes the unnoticed ones. They are not usually the athletes of the school either. Although some played sports, they were not the stars as their priorities are split with tough academic courses. Athletes have teams, ready-made groups of diverse personalities, which form a tribe, a group for each to belong to. The beautiful thing about members of a tribe is they understand each other and accept the quirks that unify them. The best way to describe the quirk that unified this group is they would be called nerds. They enjoyed puzzles, tests of logic, tricks of physics and the occasional pun. They found joy in applying the latest physics lesson to their daily life and even pointed it out as they encountered it. There is profound amazement when one discovers that algebra and the solving of triangles are meaningful when calculating the forces acting on a structure and then building that structure.

In the back of the room was a passionate, yet muffled, debate about the details of rolling dice for a D & D attribute that has 3 options since there is no common 3D object with only 3 sides, except the tricylinder[ii]. They settled on using a D6 and using 1 and 2 as 1, 3 and 4 as 2, and 5 and 6 as 3.

As the door swung open again, all anticipating eyes met Shelbi, who seemed to be on the verge of tears while simultaneously smiling. She struggled a bit on the way through the door as she pivoted her arm crutch through the opening and limped to a work table. The following eyes made her more uncomfortable, so she bowed and said, "at your service," and sat down, resting her crutch on the edge of the table, and looked at her phone.

Cody had already opened his laptop and was recording a bit of software that he had been thinking about before allowing himself to get distracted, seeing if he could load the game of Doom on a robot cortex. The world could be collapsing around him and he would remain locked on target to finish a code modification as fast as keys can click, seeming to perform better under pressure. Maybe it was just his way of escaping his home life.

Unnoticed by Cody, Griffin entered the room, wearing no shoes and a baseball cap, in a combined manner of haste and lack of concern about his tardiness. It seemed that his haste was more a function of thinking about, and working on, so many things at once, rather than getting to class.

Excited to share with Abby, his welding partner, Griffin sat down next to her and said, "I was working on my car for the last week non-stop and just welded the suspension last night. I can't believe I didn't know any of this last year and now it is almost ready to race. I just hope I don't fail this class." Griffin had an underdeveloped sense of fear, the fears that stop people as they ponder what could go wrong.

Suddenly a door opened, not the one the class was expecting. The storeroom door in the back of the class had been open ajar, but no one gave it much thought since the only things in there were materials and tools. A tall, energetic fellow with glasses dressed in a white lab coat emerged carrying lumber and some duct tape. Leaping right into conversation as if he had been talking all morning, "So, how do you build a bridge?"

To say the class was caught off-guard would be an understatement. They were still pondering the last video game they played until the early morning hours and he was asking about building bridges? Cody appeared to not even hear the question, his normal response as he was already thinking of several other things. Sitting in the front row and eager to impress her fellow classmates and new teacher was Cōngmíng de Māo, who called herself Mia for short. She was the smallest student and the only freshman in the class. In Oaks Engineering classes the upperclassmen mentored the younger students and classes often had mixed ages, she asked, "What type of bridge?" without looking up from her notes.

The tough part for any student is figuring out one's place in the dynamic social structure of high school. Act too smart and you are classified as the nerd, too popular and you are stuck up, too talkative and you could say the wrong thing, too athletic... maybe there was no problem being too athletic except the nerds won't respect you as a valuable asset in a group project. When the whole group recognizes that they were the collection of misfit toys, to begin with, they were usually more accepting of others' oddities. This group thought more about the next physics question than about how others thought about them.

Somewhat taken aback at this insightful question, the teacher stopped and turned around to see who had been so quick to think ahead.

"Is it for people, cars, or just theoretical?" Mia continued.

"Let's assume it is for people," he answered.

Interested in this sudden plunge into the practical, Griffin asked, "How long does it need to be?"

"How about 9 feet," the teacher answered.

"Bummer, plywood is 8 feet long," said Griffin, leaning forward, anxious to build this new bridge.

"Are there any other requirements?" asked Maggie quietly, who was already taking notes to make sure she did everything in the most proper way possible. Although talented in soccer, music, physics, engineering, and math, Maggie would rather step back and let others lead, yet she combined her skills with a friendly personality and compassion for others, making her one of the best leaders. She just didn't realize it yet.

"Mr. Stonebridge taught you well. You have learned well. Speaking of that, I should introduce myself. I am Mr. Alpin and will be your mechanical engineering teacher this year. One of the most important concepts that I can teach you is one you have already demonstrated. Define all the requirements first."

Mr. Alpin continued carrying the lumber to 2 workbenches and then slid the 2 benches until they were about 9 feet apart. As he placed the 2x6 on the bench, a splinter found the narrow space between his nail and finger, "Ouch!" he proclaimed and turned around with a needle of wood extending from the tip of his index finger.

Shelbi opened her backpack, produced a small box and started to limp across the room, "I've got this."

Surprised and not knowing exactly she meant, he paused. Shelbi stated matter-of-factly, "I'm first aid certified and have my kit. Let me see your hand."

Mr. Alpin was generally more comfortable doing this to himself, as he had plenty of practice, but somehow the way Shelbi said it he knew he should just let her do her job. She already had the sharp-point tweezers in hand and had sat down. She inhaled and paused, as a sniper does before pulling the trigger, and gently pulled the splinter out.

"Wow, OK. Thank you. I was not intending for a demonstration in first aid on the first day of class. Hopefully, it is our last." The class chuckled as Shelbi closed her kit and returned to her seat.

"What is engineering?" he asked and paused allowing for an awkward moment of silence. "I define it as the science of solving the world's problems. That means that the single most important thing you should get quite good at is asking the question, 'what is the problem we're trying to solve?'" He pulled a dry erase marker out of his pocket as if to write on the board but realized that he had walked to the side of the room opposite the board and slid the pen back into his pocket.

"Engineering is all about solving the world's problems, but so often people get distracted trying to solve symptoms and not the real problem. If the problem is with a 'tool,' you probably haven't found the problem yet. Let's try some examples."

Griffin, confused by this sudden offramp to discuss world problems, leaned back to see where this was going.

Mr. Alpin continued, "You are digging a hole and your shovel breaks at the handle. What is the problem?"

"Like you said, your shovel broke," stated Brent bluntly.

"Is that the real problem? The shovel is a tool to do what?" asked Mr. Alpin.

"Dig holes," said Brent.

"So, the problem is?" Mr. Alpin paused. "That you cannot dig the hole. If you had a backhoe sitting next to you when the shovel broke, you might think the shovel is rather insignificant."

"Unless you're digging in a small area and the backhoe doesn't fit so the shovel breaking is the problem," defended Brent.

"True. I am trying to help you to pull back and see the whole problem. Let's try another one. Your car breaks down on the way to school. What is the problem?"

Excited by the topic of cars, Griffin blurted, "It could be your fuel system, electrical system, ECU, any one of many sensors, or... We need more information."

"You are correct about needing more information, but I would challenge you to find the real problem, the one that is bigger than the car. A car is just a tool."

Students looked down and averted any eye contact. These are the brightest students and they were asked a simple question, if Griffin, who was building his own race car, proposed a diagnosis for a car failure and it was not the answer, then the group was stumped.

Shelbi, who normally doubted anything she would say, offered, "You need a new ride, a way to get to school."

"Exactly!" said Mr. Alpin.

Shelbi smiled.

"The key is to be able to pull back far enough to see what the real problem is so that you can find real answers. Once we identify that the real problem is actually the lack of transportation, we can find alternative solutions. If we focus on the car being disabled, we focus only on the car, merely a symptom or tool to get places."

He continued, "Let's try another one. Your GPS dies, so what is the problem?"

Without looking up, Cody pointed out, "It is a hardware issue because the software is pretty simple to triangulate from four or more satellite signals as long as you have a signal." And Griffin finished the thought, "but the real problem is that we need navigation or that we are lost."

"Yes," confirmed Mr. Alpin. "Now we can focus on getting unlost. Instead of fixing a GPS we could ask someone for help or find a map. Whenever you encounter a new problem, whether it is software, hardware, mechanical, or even social, start by asking, 'What is the real problem?' You can even apply this to social situations. Let's say a friend is saying mean things about you on social media. What is the real problem?"

"That never happens," said Shelbi with an obvious note of sarcasm.

Mr. Alpin paused but this abstract concept seemed to catch them without an answer to a common issue and said slowly, "What is the real problem if a friend is saying mean things?"

"They're not your friend," said Maggie. "The relationship is the problem."

"Ah, exactly! See how when we find the real problem, we stop running around trying to fix the wrong thing. Find the real problem and you can find a real solution. In this case, fix the relationship, right? Let's get back to building bridges."

"Yes!" exclaimed Griffin.

Mr. Alpin had placed the 2x6x10 across the span of the 2 benches and as he sat down on the flat side of the lumber a couple of the students faintly gasped. "Why did you fear? I am not that heavy, am I? Would you have felt better if I flipped it like this?" and proceeded to rise slightly to twist the board upright and then sit down again. "What's the difference? It is the same piece of wood, isn't it?

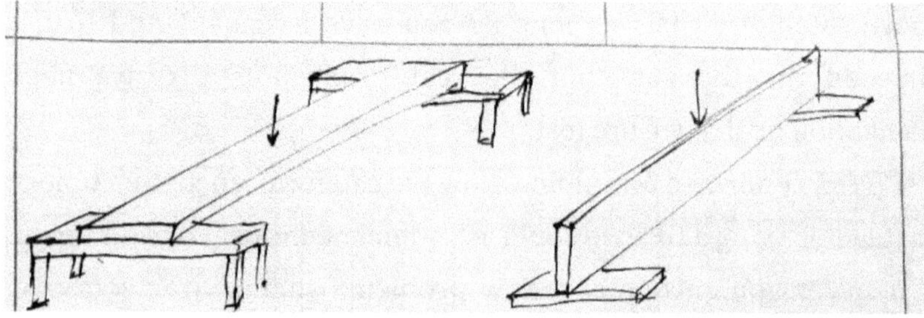

Brent spoke up from the back of the room, "It's pretty obvious. It's stronger because it is taller."

Several other students rolled their eyes, realizing that Brent hadn't changed over the summer.

He continued, "I help my dad with construction in the summers and we make ramps out of a couple 2x4s and nail some ply to the top and it ends up surprisingly strong."

"Indeed. Do you want to know the equation that explains this magic?" Looking at his phone for the time, he continued, "With our minimum day, we are out of time today, but tomorrow we will unlock the magic. Wear something appropriate to operate power tools."

"Operate power tools," Maggie said to Mia on the way out the door.

"I thought we were going to use computers in this class," said Mia. "He seems interesting... a bit crazy, but it is better than boring."

"Are you a Sophomore?" asked Maggie.

"No, a Freshman."

"How did you get in this class?"

"I am not too sure. I was at another school and have taken physics and went to some engineering camps."

"I am headed to lunch with friends. Do you want to join us?"

"I was just going to hang out and study," said Mia.

"On the first day of class? What do you have to study?"

"I, I like to read."

"Come on and eat with us, then you can read," said Maggie.

Mia found her words comforting and understanding as if she were talking to her older self. Without saying anything, she just continued to walk with her.

"Do you find it to be difficult to be a girl in engineering classes?" asked Mia as they crossed campus. "You seem to know your stuff. Do the guys accept you? I'm asking because I am coming from another school where the math and science classes were filled with boys and I was uncomfortable. I moved here because I heard it was better."

"I've known Griff, Cody, and Cable for years and we have been lab partners. I guess they accept me. It doesn't really come up. I'm just intimidated by the subject matter sometimes. I don't want to give the wrong answer," said Maggie as they approached a group of girls under a tree. "This is Quorra and Carly and this is ... Mia, right?"

"Ya, my friends call me Mia because it's tough for most people to say my Chinese name."

"Are you new here?" asked Quorra.

"Yep, I just moved here. Are you into math and science too?" asked Mia.

"I'm in Computer Science and orchestra with Maggie," said Quorra.

"I play the cello," said Mia. "Is it a fun group here? What do you play? I haven't figured out if I should play golf or cello for my last elective.

"You should definitely play music with us. I play sax and Maggie plays the violin."

"How was engineering, Maggie?" asked Carly.

Mia and Maggie chuckled a bit. "Well, the teacher seems funny, but tomorrow we are supposed to wear clothes that are appropriate to use with power tools," Maggie said as she adjusted her tone and accent as if to imitate the final instruction of the class. Quorra and Carly both laughed.

"Power tools in engineering?" asked Quorra. "What happened to Mr. Stonebridge?"

"I heard he went back to some high-paying engineering job," said Maggie. "It's a bummer. I had fun doing the solar boat team last year. I wonder if they will do that again."

After Mia had eaten quickly, she said, "My next class is Algebra 2 in Room 2718[iii]. Where is that?"

"Oh, you have Ms. Euler. Super cool. Second floor of that building, around on the other side," said Carly pointing to the building to the East.

"Thanks, I'm going to go find it."

"And read?" asked Maggie.

"Naturally[iv]. See you tomorrow. In jeans and ready to run a saw," said Mia with a smile.

CHAPTER 2 – BUILDING BRIDGES

Learning to collaborate is part of equipping yourself for effectiveness, problem solving, innovation and life-long learning in an ever-changing networked economy. - Don Tapscott

As the last of the students were making their way in the door, Mr. Alpin began, "Shall we build bridges today? First, we need to cover 10 minutes of math, so buckle up."

Moving to the side of the room with the whiteboard and pulling the marker from his pocket, Mr. Alpin wrote three equations and some sketches.

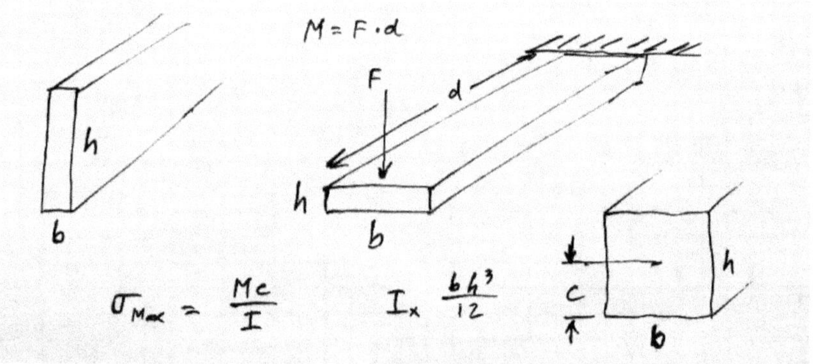

"The stress, σ, in a beam is a function of the bending moment, M, and the inverse of I_x, the moment of inertia of the cross-section. I_x is a function of the base of the cross-section rectangle and the height to the 3rd power. If you double the height, how much does the value of I_x increase?"

Maggie had been following the math and checked her answer twice and said, "2 to the 3rd power is 8, so 8 times bigger."

"Exactly, so if you want the most strength you need the tallest section. Just having many layers does not make it stronger unless you connect the layers together to make a single beam."

Mr. Alpin did several other examples and calculations. "Since we have a double block today, you will work in teams of 3-4 for an hour and make bridges that can support your weight, but you will also be weighing your bridge and the grade is a function of the weight you support divided by its weight."

About an hour later the teams were bustling about, each with its own personality. The room smelled like a lumber store as the table saw and miter saw were running feverishly and then it was mostly power drivers as the final touches were coming together.

Mia often had her face hidden in a book, but today she had a notebook and was taking notes. Mr. Alpin walked by and found she was making a list to remember everyone in her new school.

Abby – dad's a welder, 11th
Brent – 10th, construction dad, knows best
Cable – 11th, software, hardware, try anything
Carly – 12th, friend of Maggie
Chris – game addict, good ideas
Cody – software, 12th, awkward
Griffin – 12th, surfer?, mechanic, try anything
Jackson – 11th, quiet, plays football
Maggie – 12th, unsure but smart,
Quorra – 12th, friend of Maggie
Shelbi – 11th, had cancer, low self-image, first aid

"Alright, I want each team to present a few words about what they have found so far," said Mr. Alpin.

Griffin could barely contain himself and started speaking before even being called on, "We used only strips of plywood that we made on the table saw to maximize the height and only be ½" thick and then attached thin plywood to the top." The rest of his group nodded approvingly.

Cody was teamed with two younger students and they volunteered him to speak. "Hardware is not really my thing, but we used one 2x4 with plywood attached top and bottom, like an I-beam, but it is rather unstable."

Unhappy to work with others and being convinced of having the best design, a sophomore named Brent worked on his own and simply said, "I made my own I-beams out of 1x4s, so it will be the lightest."

Maggie raised her hand. "Our team calculated three designs and chose to use 2 2x4s with plywood on top, the seams furthest from the center. It will be heavier than Cody's group."

"I don't think our design will be as good as these others, but it is similar to Griff's," began Shelbi. "We used plywood for the vertical sections but had trouble joining the horizontal to vertical strips until Chris had the idea to use dowels, like screws when pinning a bone together, but we did not have enough time to finish."

"Great job everyone. Let's test them. First, on the scale," said Mr. Alpin.

Each team carried their bridge to the scale and one by one they tallied the measurements on the board.

Griffin	28 kg
Cody	33 kg
Brent	32 kg
Maggie	34.2 kg
Shelbi	29 kg

Mr. Alpin surprised them by walking across each bridge. All supported the weight; Shelbi's team bridge crackled a bit but still held. "Perhaps they were overdesigned?" he remarked as he smiled. "Brent, why do you think yours was not as light?"

"I used 1x4s which are ¾" x 3-1/2" and they used ½" plywood. I was worried about attaching the thin section to the upper sheet without splitting but I like the dowel idea that Chris had."

The teams took turns applying force with the hydraulic press until they cracked in half, some splintering all over the floor.

"Let us not compare or evaluate our accomplishment, or especially our worth, by the measurements on the scale. The true value that is measured is what we learned by the task. So, students, what did you LEARN from the process?"

"I learned that we could probably form a better design if we all contribute to and discuss a design before we start cutting wood," said Cable.

"I learned that maybe I can be too careful," said Maggie.

"I learned that I am stupid," said Shelbi, only half joking.

"Not hardly, Shelbi. Just like an author writes one word at a time and the end of the story, your story, isn't written yet. You write your story, one day at a time, so write what you want your story to be. Turn the page to a new, white sheet and write. Most people are afraid to write something new and just go back to the same story we know, even if it isn't what we want. We will pick this up next time. See you tomorrow."

As they were leaving class, Cable helped Shelbi with her backpack. "What do you think he was saying about writing our story?" Shelbi asked Cable.

"I'm not sure about much in this class," said Cable. "I haven't had physics or calc like you all have. I've just figured things out on my own. Then he says stuff about writing our story and I really don't know what he is talking about."

"It sounds like he is saying something about how we can change the outcome. I'm going through some tough stuff right now and I hope I can change my path," said Shelbi.

Cable replied, "My parents divorced when I was little and now my parents are remarried and having new kids. I guess it kind of gives me hope to think that my future is not necessarily going to be all bad and I can do something about it. It always seems like we don't have much say at our age. We are told what school to go to, what to work on, what college to apply to and it just feels out of my control sometimes. Have you noticed Chris in class? He is always sitting in the back and playing computer games on his phone. Seems like he is just trying to escape, but he has a problem."

"In class?" asked Shelbi. "I hadn't noticed. Lots of kids are into gaming. I've heard it can be an escape. I like to read and hang out with friends. Speaking of that, I am going to the quad and will take my backpack now."

"No problem. Oh, no. It's lunch. I am supposed to be at the Robotics Club meeting. Let's see what we make or break tomorrow. See you then."

Cable ran to the meeting where the other robotics students were already gathered. Mr. Alpin, Ms. Mitre and the principal were standing at the front and talking to the group. Cable glided in behind a couple of other students and took a seat on a metal stool. Cable and Cody were probably the two most significant members of the team with both hardware and software expertise and endless hours of dedicated work in the lab. The principal was talking about the last robotics season and that their team had won some special award for performance and sportsmanship and invited the team to come forward. Brent jumped up ahead of the group and received the trophy and held it while smiling while the other members came forward. Cable almost forgot to get up to receive his recognition as he seems to be driven by an internal force that does not seek praise. Brent only gave up the trophy when another member asked to look at it, but he promptly took it back before returning to his seat.

Sensing the awkwardness, Ms. Mitre said, "This team trophy will be displayed in the school trophy case until the following year." Her emphasis on the word "team" may have been imagined but regardless, its significance was lost on Brent, who said as he was leaving, "Maybe we could take turns keeping the trophy."

Maggie stood to leave and said quietly to Cable and Cody, "Great job guys. Are you headed out for lunch? I want to work on some of that physics homework before the class today."

CHAPTER 3 – FALL DANCE

For good ideas and true innovation, you need human interaction, conflict, argument, debate. - Margaret Heffernan

The fall dance was approaching, a nightmare for the socially awkward. Many would like to go but dread the process. The group of engineering students had close friendships, some that began years before and some only recently discovered. They enjoyed each other's company but tried not to overthink the situation. Most of them would end up going with someone in the same group of academic friends.

As the date of the dance approached some students planned elaborate ways to ask a date. Most students awkwardly watched the date get closer and calculated what was the minimum amount of time between asking a date and the date of the dance. The problem is that guys think that all that is needed is a suit and some flowers, but a girl is thinking about dresses, makeup, hair, and the zit that is just starting to redden on her chin. Then, there is the Hermione syndrome. Even though she is the smartest and one of the prettiest girls at the school hidden in plain sight, the boys are intimidated to ask her. Determined to go, and not willing to wait for some boy to get the courage to ask, Maggie, a senior, did not want to miss the experience. She was friends with most of the boys in the group, but

Griffin and Cody had already asked other girls, probably as a result of a spontaneous invitation. Cable was a junior, but she thought of him as a senior since they had been in common classes for years. They were in computer science class together this year. Wanting to speak his language, she devised a way to ask him and made a sign that read,

```
1 <html>
2 <body>
3 <script>
4 prompt ("Dance?");
5 if ("Yes") {give Cablecandy}
6 else {cryandeatcandyyourself}
7 </script>
8 </body>
9 </html>
```

Maggie had created the sign over the weekend, only 5 days prior to the dance. Cable was working alone in the computer lab, earbuds in and clicking away at the keyboard. Maggie and Quorra entered the lab with Maggie holding the sign. Cable was so focused on his project he failed to notice the two girls were standing at his computer until Maggie tapped him on the shoulder with the sign in front of her. Cable looked at the sign and then at Quorra, then at Maggie.

"Is this for me or did you want me to check the syntax?" he asked.

Maggie just smiled and glared at him as he pulled the earbuds out and started reading more carefully.

"Oh, this says 'dance' and 'Cable'. Wait, you are asking me to the fall dance," he blinked.

"Good job, Sherlock," joked Quorra.

"Sure," he said. "I mean, yes. That would be great."

"Then here you go," said Maggie as she handed him a small box of candy. "See you in class." She and Quorra turned and left Cable standing in the lab with the sign, box, and a dumbfounded look. As much as we would love to have things like this happen like in the movies with the right music, lighting, and scripted interaction, this was normal for actual kids trying to navigate a world of social potholes. The sign and candy were delivered, Maggie secured a date, and Cable was realizing he needed something to wear.

He sat back down, inserted the earbuds, and texted his mom.

Cable was used to this and knew he would figure it out on his own. The fact that Cable was at least 10 years older than his siblings probably contributed to the way he stepped up and took care of what needed to get done and made him more mature than any of his peers. His father lived further away, so he asked a simpler question.

"Where's a good place to buy a suit by Friday?" His dad answered with two locations without any question about what it was for.

Cable managed to stop by one of the locations on the way home, picked it out by himself and bought it, with some encouragement by the sales girl. He was ready, except for flowers.

He texted Cody that evening.

Cable found a local flower shop that had a great web page and an online ordering interface. "Done," he said to himself.

The rest of the week continued like any other for the nerds. The ones that wanted to go to the dance, and even a few who didn't, had figured out the details and were as ready as they would ever be.

The dance was best described by Cable and Cody on Monday when Mr. Alpin asked at lunch.

"Fine," said Cable.

"It was less awful than I expected," said Cody.

"Well that's good," said Mr. Alpin. "Maggie and Quorra said they had a good time, so you guys didn't mess up too bad."

The boys chuckled.

"While you are here, I need help with some programming issues we are having with a motor driver. Do you two have time?" asked Mr. Alpin.

"I have homework and a test," said Cody. "What do you need? Can I do it tonight?"

"Sure, I will show you in class before you leave. I am going to run to get some supplies now. See you later in class," said Mr. Alpin.

After Mr. Alpin left, Cable asked, "Did you hear about Chris?"

"No."

"I heard he tried to hurt himself and is not in school anymore."

Cody was silent and did not look up.

"Dude, I know we are all stressed, but could you ever do that?" asked Cable.

"Not sure. Probably not. It would hurt too much. I have to study."

CHAPTER 4 – FRICTION

There is no innovation and creativity without failure. Period. - Brene Brown

After several weeks of class and covering many new topics, Mr. Alpin sat in his office hour grading quizzes when the door opened slowly, and Shelbi peered inside.

"What's up?" asked Mr. Alpin as he detected redness around her eyes. "Can I help you?"

"I did not do well on my last quiz. That's life I guess."

"I noticed that you did not do as well as you usually do. Anything going on?"

"This last year has been rough. I was diagnosed with bone cancer in my leg; they did surgery to remove some bone, pinned the bone for strength and now I have to use the crutch. My dad travels a lot and my parents are getting a divorce," Shelbi said blankly.

"I'm so sorry. I went through my parents' divorce in my teen years," shared Mr. Alpin. "You are a strong person with great skills, talent, and heart and will come through it, but it will suck. Sorry. Find some friends that you can count on. Not a bunch of thin relationships, but a couple you can really count on. They may not be who you think are your friends now. Hang in there and don't give up." Shelbi nodded, relieved to spill some of her pent-up frustration to someone who seemed to care.

"Regarding your quiz," continued Mr. Alpin. "Can you review and retake it on Friday?"

"Yes, and thank you," Shelbi paused and looked down. "Did you know that suicide is the 3rd highest cause of death in teens?"

"Yes," Mr. Alpin paused, weighing his next words carefully. "Is there anything else you want to talk about?"

"Oh, it's not me," Shelbi reassured. "My friend has been talking about it and I wasn't sure what to say."

"Let them know you care and encourage them to get help and always know that I am available. Call 800-273-TALK. They helped me, too. Alan Turing once said, 'Sometimes it is the people no one imagines anything of, who do the things that no one can imagine.' I think that you will surprise yourself with what you will accomplish. Class is starting in 5 minutes. Let's go."

As they arrived at the engineering lab, Mr. Alpin entered through the storage room and flew into class carrying a box brimming with fanciful engineering items.

"Today we will discuss that which enables all things to go and to stop. Can you guess what I am referring to?" he paused. "Anyone? I don't mean to rub any of you the wrong way but can any of you think of the way to make things both go and stop?"

"Another pun?" asked Abby. "Friction?"

"Indeed. Friction is responsible for all action, all motion, acceleration, and negative acceleration. Understand the physics of friction and you will get traction and it will really move you."

"Ugh, another pun."

"I will prove that friction is fun. It all comes down to one equation, Friction equals the coefficient of friction times the normal force or the downward force," writing it on the board,

$F = \mu \cdot N$ or $F = \mu N$

"There it is, friction is fun. Now the challenge is to understand how to change the coefficient, the normal force and the distance at which that force acts. That's it. How do you change the coefficient?"

"Polish the surface."

"Add lubricant."

"Change materials."

"Yes, all those," confirmed Mr. Alpin. "And it is pretty obvious how you change the normal force; you don't push on it as hard or you reduce the weight. Now the tricky one. What does it mean to change the distance? If the Force of Friction is determined by μ and N, then if you multiply that force by a distance you get a Torque or resisting moment. If a door drags at the tip on the jamb or if the hinge drags on the pin, which one resists the opening more if the friction force is the same?"

"The tip of the door because it is multiplied by the length of the door and not the radius of the pin," said Cable.

"Precisely. So, if you want to exert the greatest torque, push as far away from the hinge as possible. Gentlemen, when you open a door for a lady, it is easiest if you push at the furthest edge. If you want to have the least friction, reduce your axle diameter as much as you can for the given loads. This is why watches use jewel bearings, single points of contact on the centerline of the gear axles. If the radius is zero, then what is the resulting resistive torque?"

"Zero? But is that possible?" asked Griffin.

"Not exactly zero, due to tolerances and such, but nearly zero. Alright," continued Mr. Alpin, "the lab today is to build a sled to move this 200-pound or 90-kilogram block of concrete across the parking lot. Use whatever you find in this box and your imagination to reduce the friction and you will present in one hour."

"I found some Teflon strips that I think will work well for the sled," said Brent.

"Sounds like a slick idea," said Mr. Alpin.

"Ugh," sounded several students.

Brent's group found a small pallet that was already built and added the Teflon rails to the bottom edges and then added 3 ropes to the front edge.

"We should attach the ropes to the front so that when we pull, we reduce the normal force. If we lift the front edge it will take about 15 kg per person, but it will reduce the normal force on the Teflon by half," said Griffin.

The second group found 3 wheels, only 3, though, that would support the weight. They opted to build a triangular frame and put the block nearer the pair of wheels for stability.

"If we attach 2 ropes to the front end with only one wheel, we should be able to keep it stable enough for the level parking lot," said Abby.

The two groups presented their ideas and defended their designs. Both worked, the one with wheels did better.

"Can anyone tell us why the wheels worked better?" asked Mr. Alpin.

"Rolling friction is less than sliding," said Maggie as if she were asking herself, but then answered herself, "the same force is being reacted at the small axle versus at the drag surface and the axle probably has a much lower coefficient of friction than plastic on concrete."

"Yes, well done. Before we end today, I have an important announcement. There is an opportunity to submit what is called an 'Abstract' for an engineering conference in May. I have heard that some of you were working on some unique adaptive structural controls concepts last year and in your free time. How about I get you some more resources like lab equipment and access to some experts in the field and we increase the team size to support all this and you prepare an Abstract for the conference?"

"What do we need to do to be ready?" asked Maggie.

"An Abstract is basically a summary of your research and plan of action for your project. The bulk of the testing or data can be done between now and the time of presentation. You should have completed enough to know you have something to test. I think you have a great idea and it will make an impressive presentation. You have about two weeks to prepare the Abstract. Let's start meeting after school on Wednesdays to put this together. I recommend that you seniors who have been working on this should recruit some of the young talent to form a team of about 8. Thinking about that, I have an idea. Could Maggie, Griffin, or Cody give a quick description, or your 20 second elevator pitch, about your project to see if anyone is interested?"

Both Maggie and Cody looked at Griffin, so he began, "Well, we have an idea to use piezo sensors and actuators to sense movement in structures and then using a controls circuit and some software that Cody developed to manipulate the structure to minimize damage, like in the case of an earthquake, windstorm, or if the structure were a crane, space station, or some other moving thing."

Mr. Alpin smiled, "Great job. Let them know if you want to be on the team. See you all on Wednesday."

As everyone was leaving Cody stayed behind. "Mr. Alpin," he began. "I have been reading about gaming addiction. Did you know that 41% of people who play online video games admitted that they played computer games as an escape from the real world and about 8% have an addiction?"

"That's what I have read. Can you identify with the idea of escaping your reality?" asked Mr. Alpin.

"Ya, I guess so."

"Do you realize that engineering is a way of escaping reality?"

Cody's eyebrows rose.

Mr. Alpin continued, "You get to use your imagination to create things that never existed before. You have great ideas and you will be an amazing engineer if you can get out of the game world and innovate a new world."

"You think so?" asked Cody.

"Think about innovating new forms of transportation, water filtration, construction, automation, controls systems. That is the ultimate adventure game. Let's get to the next class but come back tomorrow with 3 new ways to move the block across the room with any materials you choose."

"Speaking of materials. Some of our project materials keep disappearing. Some of us think that Brent is taking stuff home to work on his own projects. Lately, some things have even been removed from our project bins."

"I will keep a lookout. Thanks for the heads up. Have you seen any materials reappear in other groups?"

"No, that's why we think he is taking them home."

CHAPTER 5 – ELECTRICAL

What is now proved was once only imagined. - William Blake

"First things first," Mr. Alpin said as he and students were still entering the room. "The Abstract for the conference is due tonight. I know that the team has been working on it for a week and it seemed like you were about ready, but I will stay after school if you need a last review. You have done such a great job pulling it all together."

"Today we are going to spark your imagination," continued Mr. Alpin. "Since I am more mechanical, but Ms. Mitre also has a background in electrical engineering I have asked her to join us today to cover some basic circuits, current, voltage, and resistance concepts."

"First, the purpose of a circuit is to transfer energy," started Ms. Mitre. "It often starts at a battery, or other source, and then moves through a circuit based on devices and outputs to do something like rotate motors, turn on lights, or produce heat. Let's think of electricity, or more specifically current, as water flow. It flows from a high point to a low point or from high potential to low potential, across a potential difference. Like water, if there is no difference, there is no flow. In a simple circuit that would be from one battery terminal to another along a conductor or pipe. Along the way, the current or water can get squeezed down through a small space acting like a resistor or it can be made to do different things like produce light or sound, but it must keep flowing downhill back to the other terminal. There are 3 basic equations that will help with our circuit design. $V = I * R \qquad P = V * I \qquad P = I^2 * R$"

"V is potential difference, measured in Volts. The I is current, measured in amperes or Amps. R is resistance in Ohms. P is power, measured in Watts, which is energy per second. Every time the current goes through a resistor it drops some of its voltage or potential across that resistor. We can measure the potential difference and use that information to calculate the current flowing through a given resistor. Let's try a simple example. If we have a 5 Volt battery, a switch, and a flashlight bulb that has a resistance of 10Ω we would draw the circuit like this. The lightbulb is the circle with X and the squiggle is the normal symbol for a resistor. The circuit would just be drawn with the bulb, but I included the resistor, so we don't forget its impact on the system."

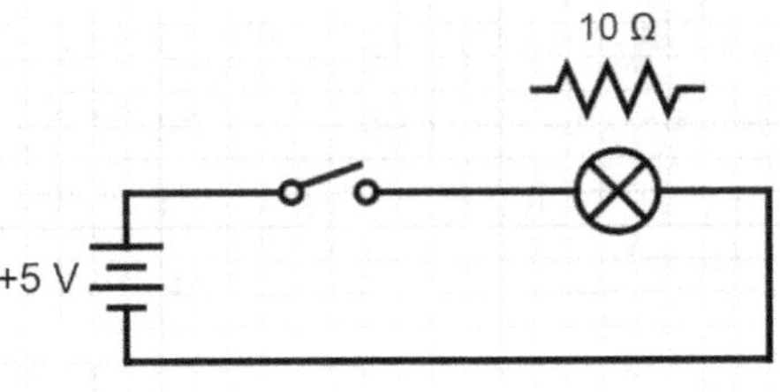

"If V=I*R, then 5=I*10, then I = .5 Amps. You can see if you increase the resistance, say using your finger as the conductor, there will be less current that can make it through the circuit, but I don't  recommend using your finger as a conductor. If you increase the voltage enough you can cause the current to flow, but it might hurt." The students chuckled.

"Let me give another quick analogy about current and voltage that has helped me think about this concept and what it means to connect things in parallel and series. Think of a battery like a water elevator or pump, some way of adding energy by lifting water up to the top of some waterfalls. The height of the waterfalls is the voltage and the width or volume of the waterfalls is the current. If we have a really tall waterfall that is the width of a pencil, it has high voltage and low current, but it is low energy. If this were directed to a waterwheel it would not turn. This is like static electricity, which is over 20,000 volts but doesn't do much except spark. If you have a waterfall that is really wide, but only a centimeter high it has high current, but low potential or voltage, again not much power. If you stack the waterfalls in series, you increase the potential difference, like a higher voltage. If you stack the waterfalls next to each other in parallel, the flow is increased, like a higher current."

"Like I said earlier, power, or energy per second, is really what determines how much a circuit gets done and how dangerous the circuit is. Power depends on both the volts, the height of the waterfall, and the amps, how much water comes over the falls. You need both to have power and turn the waterwheel. Although a car battery is 12 volts times 600 amps equaling 7200 Watts and your house might be 120 volts times only 20 amps equaling 2400 Watts, the higher voltage of the house will be able to short through your body. That's why it is pretty safe to work with low voltages in flashlights and cars, but maybe not house wiring."

"I have a box of batteries, light bulbs, and wires. I want you to try wiring the bulbs in series and in parallel and compare the light output. Remember, 'in series' means they are connected in a line and 'in parallel' means you have the current split and go in parallel through the different bulbs at once. Grab several bulbs, a battery, and some wires and try them out for the next 30 minutes."

As Mr. Alpin and Ms. Mitre walked around the room, they were watching different circuits with lights glowing dimly and some a gleaming bright white. "Why do you think some bulbs are dim and some are bright?" asked Ms. Mitre.

"Some of us just aren't as bright as others," joked Cable. "When they are in series, they are dim and get dimmer with each bulb that is added."

"Is it because we are adding resistance and with added resistance, the total current drops and the light gets less bright?" asked Maggie.

"But how does it work in parallel?" asked Mia. "What does the resistance do when we add more lights?"

"Think in terms of the water again," said Ms. Mitre. "If you had one pipe that branched into lots of parallel paths would it reduce how much goes through each pipe?"

"No, up to a point," paused Cody. "At some point, you run out of enough water to flow through the pipes, but it is not limited by the small branches, but by the supply."

"Yes," confirmed Ms. Mitre. "What you are running out of is stored charge or capacity. So, each bulb has its own resistance and will flow the same amount of current. When you add up all the currents going through the parallel branches and it exceeds what your battery or supply can provide you will see a reduction in brightness. This will work the same for other sources of resistance. So, lights, or motors, or heaters will either add more resistance if you wire in series or draw more current if you wire in parallel. If you have a limited supply and need the most light, what do you do?"

"Just use one bulb so it gets the most current," offered Jackson.

"Could you just keep adding bulbs in parallel until it causes the light to dim, then remove the last one," said Maggie.

"Indeed," said Ms. Mitre.

"One other thing to keep in mind is that when we draw a circuit, we draw a line to represent a wire and then a wiggly line to represent the resistor, but the wire itself is also a resistor and cannot be forgotten. If you are powering something that draws a lot of current, what happens to the wire?"

"$P = I^2 * R$ would tell us that if the current is large and the resistance is large then we have a large P, but I don't know what that is," said Maggie.

"Exactly right. If the wire or extension cord is too long or too thin and has a higher resistance and you draw a large current you quickly gain P or power, measured in Watts. Can anyone think of items that have outputs measured in Watts?" asked Ms. Mitre.

"Hairdryers," said Shelbi.

"And heaters," finished Griffin.

"In fact, you have turned your extension cord into a heater, and they can cause fires. So, the moral to the story is that if you need to carry a lot of current you should use a thick cord, make it as short as possible, and don't have loose connections," said Ms. Mitre.

"Tomorrow, we will work with motors and see what happens when we add drag and measure the current," said Mr. Alpin. "Please put the different parts back in the bins as you clean up. See you tomorrow."

CHAPTER 6 — LIFT AND LOFT

The true sign of intelligence is not knowledge but imagination. --
Albert Einstein

A couple of weeks later, Mr. Alpin met the class as they were arriving in front of the engineering lab. The air was not as hot as late summer but instead it was breezy with a touch of chill in the morning. Dry leaves scattering across the parking lot and a few of the students who dressed to be inside were wrapping their arms up close and Maggie pulled on a Cal Poly[v] sweatshirt.

In his usual abrupt manner, Mr. Alpin started as if in mid-sentence, "How do you make something float? Does a kite float? Does a bird float? How do wings work?"

Griffin replied, "Buoyancy, no, and only on water. What was the fourth question?"

"Well done. It was how wings work, but that is really a different topic about relative pressure on the top and bottom of an airfoil. Today we are discussing how to make things float, either in water or in air or any other fluid," started Mr. Alpin. "Does anyone know why something floats?"

"Because it's lighter than water," answered Shelbi.

"Yes. Specifically, because it is lighter than the fluid that it displaces," added Mr. Alpin. "Let's go inside, it's chilly. Have you ever thought about how a huge steel ship that is full of steel shipping containers can float on water? Surely all that steel is heavier than water, right?" He paused, then continued, "Yes, but the total displaced volume of water is so large and assuming $1000 \text{ kg} / \text{meter}^3$ or 8.3 pounds/gallon we have a lot of weight. Here is the equation." He wrote on the board.

$$F_{buoyant} = \rho V_f g$$

"The term ρV_f is the density of the displaced fluid times the volume of the displaced fluid, which is just equal to its mass, $F_{buoyant} = m_f g$ But look at that! The mass of the displaced fluid times the magnitude of the acceleration due to gravity is just the weight of the displaced fluid. So, we can rewrite the formula for the buoyant force as,"

$$F_{buoyant} = W_f \quad \text{Archimedes' principle}$$

"So, let's say we needed to move 3 people across the swimming pool in a bathtub, how would we calculate how much we could carry? Incidentally, what is the density of water at different temperatures? Did you know that it is slightly more dense at 4C than it is when it freezes? What does this unique phenomenon cause on our planet?"

Seeing mostly blank stares during this brief derailment of thought, Mr. Alpin continued, "It allows water to pack tighter and tighter into cracks in rock and then expands rather quickly as it cools from 4C to freezing at 0C causing rock to be broken down over time into smaller rock and eventually soil that can be useful for farming. Rock would only wear away at the surface if it was not for this property of water. Back to bathtubs. How about you do it this way, assume you have 3 people with an average weight of 135 pounds each. How big would a container have to be to have a 20% margin and provide the buoyancy for the group? Don't forget your container weight of 50 pounds. Although I am giving you these figures in Imperial units, convert and do your calcs in metric, it makes it easier. Work in groups or by yourself and see if you can get an answer before you sink or 5 minutes."

Six minutes later he calls out, "Any answers?"

"Sure," said Brent. "The total weight is 135x3 + 50 = 455 pounds = 206 kilos. Assume 1000kg/m³ for water, so we need .206 m³ plus 20% margin is .247 m³. If we wanted an actual shape that they could sit in we could use something that is about 1.5 m long and .4 m wide, it would need to be about .4 m tall. I think I would want it taller if there were any waves or if we were rowing."

"Super! Well done," started Mr. Alpin. "I like your observation about making it taller for practical reasons. It is not only about the perfect math but using your head. Just having the perfect volume based on math is not enough to really row your boat across a body of water. The next part of this discussion is to apply it to floatation in air. Let's use a balloon," said Mr. Alpin and then wrote on the board.

Mass of balloon = 80 kg

Volume of balloon = 1200 m³

Density of Helium = .18 kg/m³

Density of Air = 1.3 kg/m³

"Determine the total mass that can be lifted by the helium balloon."

As the students were doing their calculations Mr. Alpin paused to give them a head start and then started writing the calculations on the board.

Mass lifted = mass of the volume of fluid displaced

Mass = (1200 m³)(1.3 kg/m³)

Mass = 1560 kg

"What is the total amount that can be lifted?" asked Mr. Alpin.

"1560 kg, including balloon, helium, and payload," said Maggie

Mass of helium = (1200 m³)*(.18 kg/m³) = 216 kg

"Subtract the mass of the balloon and mass of the 1200 m³ volume of helium from the total mass that can be lifted. 1560-80-216 = 1264 kilos or 12 kilonewtons."

Mass balloon - 80 kg

Volume balloon - 1200 m³

Density He - .18 kg/m³   Mass He = 1200 × .18 = 216 kg

Density Air - 1.3 kg/m³   Mass air = 1200 × 1.3 = 1560 kg

1560 - 80 - 216 = 1264 kg

Determine the force   F = mg = 1264 × 9.8

= 12,347 Newtons

"Alright, now determine how big of a balloon you need to carry a camera that weighs 147 grams and then fill this balloon and test it. I want you to target the neutral buoyancy point such that it should just float but not drop or ascend. You only have about 30 minutes, so work efficiently."

The balloon started filling just 20 minutes later and the students were attempting to measure the length and diameter as it expanded. Cody had written a quick spreadsheet to calculate the volume of the egg-shaped balloon and they were busy revising the dimensions and confirming the volume.

	A	B	C	D	E	F
1	radius	large	small	volume	mass	
2	cm	cm	cm	meters	kg	
3	29	49	41	0.158444	0.000458	

Cell D3 formula: $=(2/3*3.14*A3*A3*(B3+C3))/1000000$

"Don't forget the weight of the balloon itself," reminded Mr. Alpin.

"We have that in the calcs, right Cody?" asked Maggie.

"Yes. I think we should be at neutral buoyancy."

Mr. Alpin brought over the camera and attached it. "Moment of truth." He let go and it hung in midair and ever so slightly rose from his hand. "Beautifully done. That was not an easy shape, not like a perfect sphere in a textbook."

"Now, please do not try to combine the concepts of today to find a way to loft 3 people into the air. I would like to keep you alive and keep my job." The class chuckled.

"I also have some amazing news," began Mr. Alpin. "Your research project abstract submittal has been accepted and our team has been invited to present its findings at the conference..."

As the group erupted in applause, he finished his sentence, "in Europe in May. You have only 6 weeks to finish compiling the data, report, graphics and get ready to go. Can you get it done?"

"Yes, no problem."

"Of course."

"Who are the final team members?"

Maggie replied, "Griffin, Cody, Cable, Brent, Shelbi, Mia, Abby, and me."

"Terrific! Usually, this conference is not attended by schools, as you know. Usually companies and agencies like NASA and ESA present at these, so the schedule is a bit awkward with school and finals. What I heard from my friend on the NASA committee is that they were so impressed with your research and innovative thought that they want to hear your findings. You need to reach out to your teachers and see who can go. I will back you up, but you need to finish assignments early, negotiate how to finish your classes and finals. I have some other things to talk about, so the 8 of you need to stay for a minute and the rest are dismissed. See you tomorrow."

"The school will help cover some travel costs for up to 8 of you. Speaking of the 8 members of the team, I have something planned for you in a few weeks. I am putting together an engineering retreat for this team. We will do some team-building, I know," he defended, looking at the questioning looks on their faces, "not your favorite thing for a couple of you. We will also cover all sorts of engineering concepts, but in the outdoors. I am taking you camping. I will email all the details tonight. Great job team, super proud of you. See you tomorrow."

CHAPTER 7 – LIFE

If you have always done it that way, it is probably wrong.
- *Charles Kettering*

Maggie, Quorra, and Carly were all sitting near the practice field enjoying the sun during their last period, a change from their normal spot on the couches in the math pod. Their conversation flitted from one homework problem to another to short group-processing of social situations. The football team began filing out onto the field for practice. The girls continued talking, uninterested in the blocking and defending drills that were progressing until their friend Jackson squared off with another player about the same size, Jackson was hit and he flew backward on the turf, landing on his back a few feet in front of the girls making the sound of a heavy sack of grain being dropped, *whoomph.* "Are you OK?" asked Carly.

"Ya, it always happens," moaned Jackson.

"Well, your center of gravity was too high for your stance," replied Quorra.

"Do you play football?" asked Jackson.

"No, but your physics is all wrong," replied Maggie. "Your feet are too close together and you are standing too tall to try to block."

"Try leaning into it at the last second before contact to shift your center of gravity and increase momentum," offered Quorra.

"Or step aside just before he hits you next time," Carly said half joking.

"Are you serious?" asked Jackson.

"Yes, we're serious," replied Maggie. Your center of gravity is just about where your belly button is and if that gets moved outside of your virtual footprint you will fall over. And it will help if you speed up to increase your momentum just before contact. Sort of do a lunge at the last second."

"What's my 'virtual footprint'?

"Jackson, are you getting back into practice or hanging out with the girls?" yelled the coach.

"It's the perimeter of where you are in contact with the ground," yelled Maggie as Jackson ran back to the center of the field.

They watched as he lined up for the next drill. He glanced over at them as if asking them if they knew what they were talking about. Carly nodded.

After the whistle and crash of pads and helmets, Jackson was still standing. As a matter of fact, he had pushed his opponent back over the line. He looked over to the girls in disbelief.

"Physics," said Maggie.

"Basic physics," replied Quorra. All three smiled.

"I have to run to a meeting now," said Maggie as she stood to go.

Meanwhile in the computer science pod of the engineering lab, after a brief discussion about the speed difference of a While loop vs an If statement, Cody directed the conversation to solving the position controls for the robot arm so that it won't have a null pointer error. Cable offered one solution after another. It is always fun to watch two amazing brains discussing things that make no sense to anyone else in the room, but they passionately propose, dismantle, and confirm solutions.

Generally, innovators have little time for small talk and prefer to focus on the present and interesting world and many are not shy to express their boredom with topics or people who do not capture their attention. This could be considered rude by more social types, but it is just being efficient with conversation.

The conversation became loud and energetic again as they brainstormed aloud about using Rust programming language to control the robot cortex. "It uses concurrent processing and highly efficient memory management while maintaining memory integrity and its safety is unparalleled," said Cody.

"Ironic that the processing is parallel, but it is unparalleled," finished Cable.

Although secretly pleased by the comment, Cody did not want to show his amusement and looked back to his laptop. "Let's finish this autonomous sequence before the meeting," said Cody. "I need it quiet for a minute while I decide if it is better to use absolute or relative indexing for the arm."

"Wouldn't it be better to use absolute, so we don't accumulate an error?" asked Cable.

"We would compare the starting location to absolute each time anyway and then either give it an absolute or relative command, but I am worried that the absolute will end up in an infinite loop trying to achieve a perfect location. That's why I need to think, alone."

Cable understood it was time to stop offering solutions and let him think. Each programmer operates in their own way. Some prefer to diagram the process, some prefer dialogue, and some will visualize the program in their head, seeing each loop and path as if they were roller coaster tracks that lead to different outcomes. The silence would be awkward, it seems to be asking to be filled with conversation, but silence between two brilliant minds is merely its own While loop:

While contemplating all these possible algorithms,

Do nothing else, until the best solution is found.

Engineers understand that one is always searching for the best solution. It is not the end solution, but the best at the given time with the given resources. With more time or resources there are infinite better solutions. One trick to becoming a good engineer is balancing the desire to find the best solution and to complete the task. Some engineers error to either extreme and will continue in the While loop and never complete anything or will want to rush to a conclusion too soon without evaluating all the possibilities.

"Relative control," stated Cody as he nodded to himself. "I can overcome the negatives and I like the advantages. Let's finish now." The conversation transformed into mostly keystrokes with an occasional comment to streamline the design. 10 minutes later they were compiling the code and testing and about 15 minutes after that it was declared, "Ready for the tournament. The meeting is here after 7th period, right?"

"Yep," said Cable. "That's about now in the main room."

8 students filed into the engineering lab promptly at 3:20. The normal assortment of vehicles, projects, tools, and materials were in their usual place, but in the middle of the lab was a tent. Mia was already in the room, wearing noise ear muffs, the type you use when operating loud equipment though there was nothing operating. She was just walking around wearing them as others were chatting.

"What do you think about staying in a tent in the woods?" asked Shelbi.

"I am sure it is pretty and everything, but not really my scene," said Cody.

"What are you talking about? This is going to be great!" exclaimed Brent.

"Sit down you Boy Scout," said Shelbi.

In a rather loud voice, Mia said, "These are great. I should wear these all the time. I love how I don't hear anyone."

Normally that comment might seem strange or antisocial and elicit comments about how odd she is but in a group of engineers the response is different.

"Are there more?" asked Cody. "I want to try." He found another pair and soon both were in their own worlds of silence, just the way they liked it.

About the time that Griffin and Abby walked in, Mr. Alpin suddenly appeared from under the flap of the tent. Mia and Cody removed the ear muffs.

"Valuable lesson is that fabric does not stop sound," said Mr. Alpin. "Don't forget, on Friday we are leaving for the Oaks Engineering retreat and outdoor adventure. You have been working hard to get ready to go to Prague in a few weeks so this should be fun. I have everyone's forms except for Cable. The packing list is posted but don't forget boots, jacket, and sleeping bags. We leave right after school on Friday, because it is April and we have a 4-hour drive we will arrive after dark. Any questions?" asked Mr. Alpin.

"Do we need to bring any food?" asked Mia.

"You will need to bring your 10 Essentials on the list and one of those is enough snacks to cover you in case of an emergency for a day. The regular meals are taken care of. Be sure to read those lists and come prepared. We don't have engineering class that day so email me if you have questions. See you Friday after school."

CHAPTER 8 – ENGINEERING RETREAT

Going to the woods is going home, for I suppose we came from the woods originally. But in some of nature's forests, the adventurous traveler seems a feeble, unwelcome creature; wild beasts and the weather trying to kill him, the rank, tangled vegetation, armed with spears and stinging needles, barring his way and making life a hard struggle. - John Muir

Nervously shifting on her feet and looking at her phone, Maggie was checking her lists and trying to convince herself this experience would be fun. Abby, Griffin, and Brent were comparing equipment and sharing stories of past camping adventures. Cody was typing on his phone. Shelbi was making her way from her mom's car, Cable and Mia ran over to grab things from her.

"Let's pack up," Mr. Alpin said as he and Ms. Mitre pulled the school van into the parking lot.

The ride was uneventful, a mixture of discussion topics, music, singing, napping, and sending the last social media posts for a few days. Pulling into the camp Mr. Alpin said, "We are here. The tents are set up so just roll out your stuff. Remember to fluff up your sleeping bags to increase the insulative factor and then meet at the campfire ring that is over there when you get done," gesturing to the center of the camp.

The air was crisp, downright freezing for those who were used to Southern California. The fir and pine trees spoke swishing secrets high above the camp, and the crickets replied from the manzanitas and dogwoods below. Griffin and Cable had both dressed in shorts, it was warm back at school, and now were racing to get their gear in a tent and find their jackets and jeans.

As they started to gather at the fire ring, the trees whispered to each other. Mr. Alpin was standing in front of where the fire would be, then called for Cable and Brent to gather with the group. He said softly, "Listen. Listen to the forest. What does it tell you?"

"There is a breeze," said Shelbi but unsure.

"Yes, but listen to all your senses. What do you smell, feel, taste?"

"What does this have to do with engineering?" asked Brent.

"Everything. Engineering is about solving the world's problems, but we have to listen for the problems AND the resources. What is the world telling you?"

"I smell wet dirt," said Mia.

"I hear water flowing," said Cable.

"Indeed. We are near a stream, a source of water. Is the sound of water just low rumbling or does it have high-frequency swishing?" asked Ms. Mitre.

"I hear both low and the swishing," said Mia.

"That is important because low rumbling means that it is more distant, and the high-frequency sound is absorbed, but if you hear both it is close by. What else?" prompted Ms. Mitre.

"There is a bit of mist on my face," said Maggie.

"I hear animals. Crickets, an owl, and I think a coyote when we were moving into the tents," said Griffin.

"I feel cold and getting colder," shivered Mia.

"Let's start this fire and have some s'mores," offered Ms. Mitre.

As the fire crackled and sparks rose into the black infinity above, fingers became sticky with the sweetness of s'mores. The fire began to collapse, and conversation slowed as their gaze melted into the orange coals. The group was gathered close to the fire ring and warming their hands. Other sounds had faded away except for a distant owl that called to the deaf trees. A coyote howled and Shelbi shivered.

"Note the direction of the breeze before we head off to bed," started Mr. Alpin. "Now that the sky is black, we can see the stars and maybe the Milky Way. Where is the sound of the creek? Which way is north?"

"The creek is over there," gestured Brent as he pointed. "And north would be where the north star is."

"There is the Big Dipper," said Maggie, "and the front 2 stars point to the north star, right? There, there is the north star."

"Good," said Ms. Mitre, "so if that is north then what direction is the creek?"

"West," said Griffin.

"See how we are assembling a map from what we can hear from our surroundings? We have determined where north is, and that the creek is flowing to our west. We know we are in the western Sierra and the general direction of the slopes are to the west. Can we confirm that downhill is indeed to the west from here? One more hint is that diurnal, or daily, breezes generally flow up canyon when the sun is up and down canyon when the sun is down."

"Yes," said Cable, "because we can see more stars lower on the horizon to the west, that is downhill where the stream is, and the breeze is flowing that way too."

"Exactly right, use the data around you to understand the environment and requirements. Well done. Sleep well. We will wake up at first light and get out of our tents when the sun strikes them." Said Mr. Alpin.

"What time will that be?" asked Maggie.

"Does it matter?" asked Mr. Alpin enthusiastically. "We are in mountain time now, not clock time. Good night."

The cold blackness dropped like a heavy curtain as everyone moved to the tents and snuggled deep into their sleeping bags for the night. A low murmur continued from the tents for less than 30 minutes as the chill and darkness closed in for the night.

The first light of the day was greeted with the chirping of birds. *tweeeeet- a- dee- dee* the call of the black-capped chickadee bounced from tree to tree. The chill pierced the tent and pricked the tips of their noses and ears, making it tough to get out and get dressed, but the smell of bacon and coffee proved encouraging enough.

With the clatter of stoves, metal pots, and silverware and the sizzle of bacon, students began gathering around the table and serving themselves hot cocoa and coffee.

"What's the plan for today?" asked Maggie.

"The plan," started Mr. Alpin, "is to learn from our surroundings, work together, and have fun in this beautiful place. First, we have breakfast and a lesson in heat transfer."

As Mr. Alpin placed sausages into a pan and heard a sizzle, he said, "See how we are trying to transfer heat energy from the fuel of the stove to the sausage. How can we improve the flow of the heat?

It is all about increasing the contact area, increasing the ambient temperature, and increasing the surface area-to-volume ratio. What can we do?"

"Flatten the sausage or cut it lengthwise."

"Cover it."

"Yes," confirmed Mr. Alpin. "Anything else? How about to lubricate the process?"

"Add water?" offered Shelbi.

"Excellent," said Mr. Alpin. "Yes, add water to provide a hot media to transfer the heat and then cover it to allow the steam to heat the sausage and cutting it does increase the surface area and cutting it lengthwise increases the contact area with the pan. It gives new meaning to cooking when you apply the physics, right? Also, speaking of water, what do we need to do to prepare water to drink if we gather from the creek?"

"Filter or boil it," answered Brent.

"Yes, boiling will kill anything that will make us sick. Now, we are making breakfast burritos so is it better to use a thin steel plate or a thicker aluminum pan if we want to have even heat on the tortillas."

"Aluminum is a great conductor and if it is thicker it will distribute the heat best. I help out cooking at home a lot," said Cable.

"Correct. Well, let's finish cooking and eat," said Ms. Mitre.

After breakfast and cleaning up, the group gathered for instruction. "First, let's pair up. Everyone find a partner. Each group grab one handkerchief. Put it over your partner's eyes. Yes, even you Cody. Does every group have one blind person and one guide?" He paused and looked at each group. "The goal will be to navigate to the creek. Do you want to try to do this blind or with your guide?"

"I don't want to go swimming or tripping over the branches of that wicked gray thorny bush," grumbled Cody.

"Yes, that is Whitethorn or Ceanothus and it bites. OK, let's do it with guides. This is harder than you think. Guides, your partner does not see what you see. You need to remind them to step up or duck to avoid branches. Just to keep it challenging, you cannot touch or hold your partner, only use your voice to guide them to the creek.  Also, use your senses. Listen for the creek. Smell the plants and soil."

The pairs of students gradually made their way toward the creek. Some were quiet, a couple were yelling at each other. Some were tripping, others walking slowly and methodically.

"Ouch! Cody, why didn't you tell me to duck?" yelled Brent.

"Maybe I didn't want to," he replied, and the others laughed.

Eventually all 4 groups arrived at the creek. "Was that harder or easier than you expected?" asked Ms. Mitre.

"Harder. The branch was definitely harder than my forehead expected," grumbled Brent.

"Now let's switch roles," began Mr. Alpin. "Those that have just been guided should have a better awareness of what it takes to be a good guide. See if you can get back to camp faster and safer than the first trip."

The pairs moved faster. Cable and Griffin were almost at a jog. The ones who were blindfolded seemed to know how to walk, high, flat-footed steps, after watching their partners the first time. The guides knew how to give clear instruction. Arriving back in camp, they found treat bags with sour gummy worms, jerky, nuts, and dried fruit waiting for them.

"We are taking a 5-mile hike to a lookout and will return after lunch. What does each person need to bring?" asked Ms. Mitre.

"Lunch."

"Jacket."

"Phone?" asked Cody with a hint of sarcasm which the group responded with a collective roll of their eyes.

"Code-e, you will have to leave your computer this time," said Maggie.

"Why do you call me Code-e?"

"Hel-llooo. You are always writing code, so it just fits," said Maggie.

"I often like my computer more than people," said Cody.

"Same," said Brent.

"Water," said Mia, bringing the discussion back to the point.

"All 10 Essentials, duh," said Brent sarcastically.

"Indeed," replied Mr. Alpin. "All 10. Think of them as the 10 protections. Protection from hunger, thirst, cold, darkness, sun, and getting lost. Speaking of that, here are your maps of the area."

"Remember from last night, where is north? Orient your map with respect to north."

"The stream was to the west, so north is that way," gestured Cable.

"Look to the high peaks around us," started Mr. Alpin. The ones to the north are showing their face to the south, toward the sun. Notice the fewer trees, the grayer foliage of the manzanitas and

Ceanothus. Now, turn around and face the peaks to our south. Those slopes are facing north and are dark with heavy tree coverage and see the frost near the top of the ridge? If you are looking for warmer clines you want that slope to our north, but if you want more tree coverage and berries you want to be on the slope to our south. The outdoors is our engineering laboratory for the day. Understand the rules and innovate the solutions. Let's get ready to leave for the hike in 15 minutes."

As they drove to the trailhead, Mr. Alpin slowed and turned onto a dirt road. After a few minutes of bouncing around, they came to a flat clearing.

"Come see the view and where we are hiking to," said Mr. Alpin.

The group exited the van and stretched and then scampered up a rocky dome with an incredible view.

"You can see to our north, the Needles," said Mr. Alpin. We will be approaching them from the trailhead to the west of the peaks. Let's get to the trailhead."

The hike wound its way around a couple of small peaks and arrived at several rock spires with a lookout on the first. Eating lunch at the summit they enjoyed the view. Lessons about the mountains, the weather, the plants, and animals were woven through the fabric of the day.

Upon returning to camp, Mr. Alpin and Ms. Mitre had one last challenge for them.

"Now you need to build a shelter," said Ms. Mitre.

"How big? For how many people?"

"For what type of weather?"

"Using what materials?"

"Any other requirements?"

"You are asking all the right questions," said Mr. Alpin. "For 2 people, our current weather, cool but no snow or rain, made from anything dead and down, and build it in a safe location with easy access to water. You have about an hour, work together."

Mr. Alpin and Ms. Mitre sat in canvas chairs in camp, chatting and enjoying the forest. The team was building, but more importantly, they were planning and then building. Sketches were being drawn in the dirt. Students were holding branches in the air to simulate some structural detail or connection while conversation continued as they built.

"Watch how they are working together," remarked Ms. Mitre to Mr. Alpin. "They identified the requirements, examined their environment, chose building materials, assigned roles and tasks and now are working on some of the structural details."

"Nothing beats this place to simplify life and put the lessons to practical application, now" replied Mr. Alpin with a smile. "I wonder who will be brave enough to spend the night in it."

After about an hour, Mr. Alpin approached and said, "Design review time. Each person should share an element of the design and give the reason it was chosen."

Griffin began, "We started off using this large leaning tree as the central spine. We knew that the ridge would carry the greatest load, so it would need to be the largest beam and it was easier to find one rather than moving one."

"The next level is using the larger branches we could find to form joists," said Brent.

"We angled the entrance a bit because the nighttime airflow will be going downhill and we did not want that to blow into the entrance," said Abby.

"We covered the large branches with the willow branches from near the creek because the flat leaves form a better shell than the pine and fir needles," said Shelbi proudly.

"Then we covered the floor with dry pine needles to provide insulation from the cold ground," said Maggie.

"Then who is going to sleep in it?" asked Mr. Alpin

3 hands shot up. "Then you work out who will get to sleep in it and let's get started on dinner. Any guesses on how long until we lose the sunlight?"

A couple of students started to reach for their phones to check the time. "Not that way. Remember our time is determined by the sun, not by a clock out here. If you spread your fingers a bit and stretch out your arm, count the number of finger-widths between the sun and the ridge to the west and then from the ridge to the virtual horizon. Each finger is about 15 minutes, each hand is about 1 hour until we lose direct sunlight and then the horizon is when it gets dark."

"We only have about an hour and a half until it gets dark," said Shelbi, pleased with her new time-keeping device.

"Before we can have a delicious dinner of BBQ and roasted potatoes, we need to talk about starting a fire with limited resources," said Mr. Alpin. "You need to gather dry fuel of different sizes. If it has been raining recently, but not the current day, try smaller fuels because they dry out faster. If it has been dry but recently started raining, try larger fuels since they will still be mostly dry inside. If the fuels are generally wet, start with the driest twigs you can and then stack your future wood around the fire to get it drying out on the exterior. Anyone care to offer to build our fire tonight and tell us why you do what you do?"

"I will," said Brent. "I do the log cabin style since the teepee falls over, but I build a mini teepee inside the log cabin to get it going. The log cabin works best because it allows the air to come in from all sides."

"That is the critical element," said Mr. Alpin. If the fire does not get a steady flow of air it will struggle. People build fires in rings of rocks and it makes the rocks black, and it also starves for air and must alternate between exhausting heat up and pulling air down into the fire ring. Can anyone describe the thermodynamics and heat transfer of a fire?"

"Most of the heat goes up," said Cable, "so you have to put the fuel above the source of the flame."

"Right. What are a few ways to start a fire without a match or lighter?" asked Ms. Mitre. Several answers were given as Brent was stacking up his kindling.

"Magnifying glass."

"String and bow."

"I heard you can use a 9-volt and steel wool."

"True," said Mr. Alpin, "but how often do you have either when you are camping? Also, most flashlights have a AAA or AA battery with an LED and the 1.5 volts is too low to spark and the LEDs don't make heat or use focusing lenses. One thing I always carry when backpacking is a bag of dryer lint and a small flint and my multitool, like this."

Mr. Alpin pulled out a small bag and pinched a tuft of lint out of the bag and demonstrated using a knife to get a spark. "Do you want to give it a try, Brent?"

"Sure," said Brent as he tucked the lint under the corner of the log cabin and started drawing the knife down the flint. Sparks popped from the blade and as he adjusted the pressure and angle of the blade the sparks dazzled, popped, and flew into the lint. Small sparks danced in the fuzz and then poof, there was a flame. Brent expertly added a few pine needles while exhaling a column of air right to the small fire. One by one the twigs and stems lit, and the fire filled the frame of wood that he had built. Everyone gathered close and extended their hands to the warmth. They added logs and enjoyed the heat, cracked jokes, and laughed together.

"This has been better than I thought," shared Shelbi. "Our family doesn't do stuff like this. My parents are getting a divorce, so things are a mess right now."

"Sorry to hear that," comforted Maggie.

The fire gradually reduced to a hot bed of coals that seemed to breathe and the voices tapered to listen to the night. Mr. Alpin softly said, "Tomorrow morning will be about the same, but we will pack up after breakfast and then be heading back. You have all done so well and been good sports about living in the woods for a couple days."

Dawn emerged with glowing pink and orange skies and an icy breeze and a few clouds. The birds were quieter than usual as the students were emerging from their cocoons. Coffee was already steaming on the camp stove. Brent was crawling out from the shelter of branches.

"Pancakes and bacon in 10 minutes," called Mr. Alpin.

"It's colder this morning," said Griffin. "I need shoes today."

"Yes, most people need shoes every day in the mountains," said Ms. Mitre. "Come and get it while it is hot."

As everyone gathered and filled their plates and warming their hands on their cups of coffee and cocoa, Mr. Alpin asked, "Does anyone notice the difference this morning?"

"It's early and cold?" said Mia.

"It is colder, and the sky is colorful," said Brent.

"And there is a stronger breeze," added Maggie.

"Yes," said Mr. Alpin, "and do you know why? What is different?"

"The weather is changing," said Abby.

"Exactly, there is a cold front coming. That can mean several things in the mountains. It starts with a chill, with pink and orange skies and the wind can suddenly pick up. At this elevation, it can change to snow or hail or just be a clear and cool day. The thing to note is your day may change, so be ready. After breakfast, let's break camp and pack and then do a hike to the waterfall on the drive home so that we are ready for anything."

Camp was filled with the sounds of tent stakes being tapped together to remove wet earth from them and shaking out tarps, accompanied by joking and laughter. They also hadn't learned that canvas does not stop sound, or they just did not care.

"It wasn't as bad as I thought it would be," said Cody.

"What were you expecting?" asked Cable.

"Outside is not my friend and I miss my computer."

"Your parents never took you camping?" asked Cable.

"Just cuz my parents are Mexican?" joked Cody. "My dad works as an accountant during the day and another job at night to afford to send me and my sister to school. My mom works weekends as a nurse. They don't have time to go camping. All the pressure is on me to go to university. My dad is really strict."

"Wow, I never realized," said Cable.

"I never thought I would learn about nature and plants and weather in engineering," said Shelbi, bringing the conversation back.

"It kind of makes sense, though," said Mia. "This is just the environment we are engineering in."

Within an hour all the gear was packed away in the van and they headed for the waterfall. While driving along the ridgetop roadway the van suddenly pulled into a random dirt shoulder barely wide enough for a vehicle and Mr. Alpin announced, "We're here."

"Here? What's here?" asked Griffin. "I don't see any waterfall, or water, for that matter."

"Come along," said Ms. Mitre.

Once outside the van, the students realized it was still cool and the pines were swaying a bit in the breeze and they ducked back in to retrieve their jackets.

"Listen. What is the forest telling you?" Mr. Alpin asked, it was his favorite line of the trip.

"Wind."

"Yes, and what else?"

"There are white, puffy clouds on the ridge to our west," said Brent.

"How do you know it is the west?" asked Mr. Alpin.

"It is late morning so the sun is roughly to our south and a bit east so that would be west," he said as he pointed to the ridge.

"I hear water," said Shelbi, "but I don't see any."

"Let's go find it and follow it," said Mr. Alpin.

As they wound their way through the trees, steadily dropping in elevation they entered onto a large flat rock area and could clearly hear the stream now. In the rocks were large oblong depressions that were filled with water, but no flowing water. The creek was still 50 meters lower. Suddenly they realized they were standing in an ancient kitchen; the rock was covered in small Native American grinding holes. The creek was flowing to their south and trees shaded the kitchen area.

"Close your eyes and imagine this rock a few thousand years ago," started Ms. Mitre. "Women were gathered on this rock grinding acorns in these holes. It was more than a work area, it was a social center. Notice that it had everything they needed. Water, which also brought animals, who were in search of a drink. The oaks grow along this canyon and other plants are plentiful for shelter, firewood, and even the willows grow at the banks of the creek and they can make tools from the branches. Let's follow the creek to see where it goes."

"What does this have to do with engineering?" asked Cody.

"These are ancient engineers," said Mr. Alpin. "We can learn a lot about how they chose their living area and used their resources. Watch your step, it gets slippy here."

"Slippy?" mocked Brent.

"It's a Bear Grylls expression for slippery and I like it," replied Mr. Alpin.

After about 10 minutes of meandering through the trees along the creek, Mr. Alpin paused and asked, "Do you see or hear anything different?"

The students had been focused on not tripping and looked up and around. "There appears to be a clearing ahead because I see fewer trees downstream," said Brent. "And the white puffy clouds are turning gray."

Shelbi was the slowest to move through the brush with her crutch, but others were helping her and just as they joined the group Mr. Alpin said, "We are almost there."

A moment later and the forest dropped away and suddenly the group was standing on a granite shelf looking at the tops of the trees below. The waterfall was barely noticeable because they appeared to be standing over it.

"Whoa!" exclaimed Cable.

"Follow me," said Mr. Alpin.

"I will stay here," said Shelbi. "I don't think I want to come back up that slope."

After a few minutes of scrambling down the steep slope and clinging to the side of the granite, the group found themselves behind the waterfall. It cascaded over their heads and out to the rocky canyon below and they were looking through the sheet of water and spray with its rainbow of color.

"Is it any mystery why the native people chose this creek to live near?" asked Ms. Mitre.

"They had quite a view and a kitchen with all the modern conveniences," joked Mia.

"Let's head back up with Shelbi to take a group photo and then we better get out of this canyon before those black clouds get overhead," said Mr. Alpin.

The group scrambled back up the canyon, took photos, and were just getting back to the grinding rock when thunder rolled across the ridge. Without saying a word, the whole group picked up speed and raced for the van. The drops started hitting the dirt, *thbt....thbt.thbt,* and were speeding up just as they jumped into their shelter.

"That came up fast," said Abby.

"In the mountains, you have to watch for storms, they brew quickly and can be hidden behind the ridge," said Mr. Alpin. "Up here you get the compression of the clouds and moisture at the ridges. What's just a warm cloud in the hot valleys below gets compressed up here and if it lines up perpendicular with the ridge you have orographic compression, so the moisture condenses and falls out as rain or hail. Now we will head back home."

The students peered out the windows as the rain pelted the van and the lightning flashed. Within 20 minutes the clouds parted and revealed sparkling trees and green grasses as they descended from the ridge and into the foothill oaks. Most were asleep by the time they snaked their way through the golden grass hills that were dotted with oak trees. Mia, of course, was reading again, occasionally looking outside at the passing cows.

CHAPTER 9 — MECHANICS

Exploration is the engine that drives innovation. Innovation drives economic growth. - Edith Widder

"The conference is a few weeks away and we have a few more topics to cover. Are you ready to present your paper?"

"We are almost ready. The hardware is ready. The data is tabulated, and we are working on the paper and presentation materials now," said Maggie.

"Great job, everyone," said Mr. Alpin. "Let me know if there is anything you need from me as you get it put together. Let's talk mechanics."

"Sounds like my kind of topic," said Griffin.

"This about how stuff works, not just cars. Let's talk about a lever first. What do you use a lever to do?" Mr. Alpin asked while drawing a simple lever and pivot on the board.

"To pry things apart," answered Brent.

The door swung open and a pretty girl with shiny, jet-black hair walked in.

The class stirred, eyeing the stranger as she tried to stay invisible and make her way to a seat at the back of the lab.

"Isn't that Bekah Milano," whispered Maggie.

"Do you have the wrong building? The theater arts building is that pretty one on the other side of campus," said Brent in a tone that acts like a sharp object being drawn across your hand and you aren't sure if it cut so you squeeze it to see if blood oozes out. "Why are you here?" he squeezed.

"Well, that didn't take long," said Bekah confidently with a bit of a Mediterranean accent. "Have you ever felt out of place? I have always wanted to be an engineer, so I am in the engineering program and started here today. Thanks for the warm welcome."

"Welcome," said Mr. Alpin, who felt the sudden chill in the room and was trying to figure out why this new student looked familiar. "We are discussing mechanics, specifically levers."

"We have a lever with 10 cm on the left side of the pivot and 100 cm on the right. If we want to lift 500 kilograms on the left, how much force do we need on the right?"

$$500 \times 10 = F \times 100$$
$$F = 50$$

"Isn't it like a ratio?" asked Mia

"Yes, we can set it up as force times distance on the left equals force times distance on the right, so 10x500 = F x 100. Then F is 50. If we could move the pivot really close to the load that we are lifting what does the required force do?"

"Goes down," said Griffin. "I used something like this to lift the engine out of my car."

"What if we wanted to keep something moving and had a series of levers all on the same pivot?" Mr. Alpin asked as he drew a series of levers and then drew two circles that represented gears.

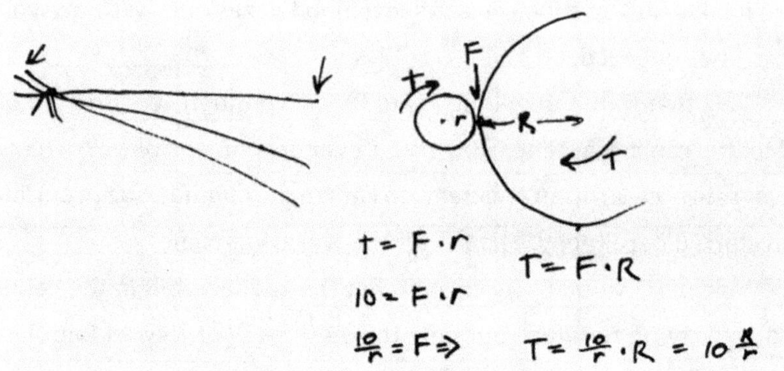

"If we have a small gear on the left with radius 'r' and the large gear with radius 'R' and then apply a torque of 10 Newton-meters on the left what torque is required to balance the equation on the right? We can solve F in terms of r and substitute. The torque on the right is just the input torque times the ratio of the gear sizes. It is a series of levers that amplify the torque. Remember that gears can only amplify the torque or the speed but never both, so if you figure out that the gear set is doubling the speed then it is half the torque. One way to remember it easily is if you rotate a large gear once how many times will it rotate a small gear that is 1/10th the size?"

"10 times?" proposed Maggie.

"Yes, so then the torque must do what?"

"1/10th the torque," said Bekah, surprised faces turned her way. Cable looked at Bekah and Maggie glared at Cable.

"Exactly. Now let's add some rope to the equations. Say we have a rope that goes over a pulley wheel and it has 15 kilograms hanging

on one side. How much do we need to pull on the other side of the
pulley to keep it balanced?"

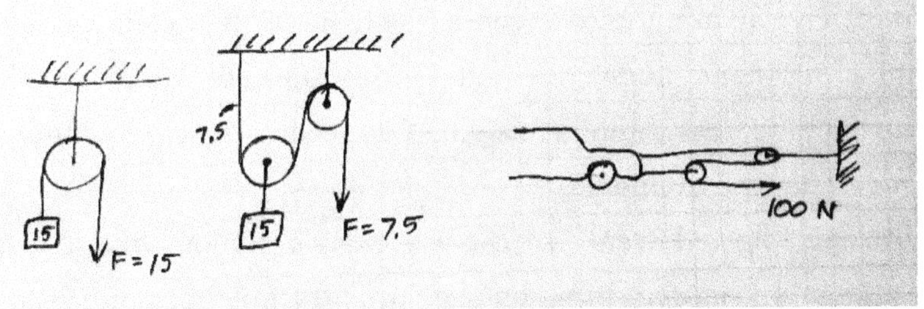

"15," said Cable.

"Yes, but don't forget that the 15 kilograms is a mass and the force
would need to be times 9.81 for Newtons. How much is the total
force on the bracket that supports the pulley?" asked Mr. Alpin as he
paused for an answer. "Remember to add up the forces. How many
total pulling down?"

"15 for the mass plus 15 pulling down, so 30, times 9.81 needed
going up," said Abby.

"Yes. That is if we are only redirecting the same load. Now here is
a harder one. If we loop the rope over a pulley and attach it back to
the ceiling what happens?"

"The 15 kilograms would be divided evenly between the 2 ropes,
7.5 each which goes over the pulley so about 75 Newtons," said Cody.

"How about if we need to pull a car out of the mud and we can
pull with 100 Newtons and have 2 pulleys, how much force can we
generate?" asked Mr. Alpin.

"If we attach the rope to the car and then out to a tree and back
to another pulley at the car, we can get 3 ropes that are pulling on
the car. Wouldn't that be 300 Newtons?" asked Griffin.

"Yes, now you have a way to get your car out," confirmed Mr.
Alpin. "Note that you can keep adding loops if you have pulleys. In

the real world, each pulley has friction and will take away some of your pulling force, but you can multiply your force quite a bit."

"You have 30 minutes to devise a way to lift my truck and get that dummy out from under the axle!" Mr. Alpin exclaimed while gesturing to his truck that no one had noticed had a crash dummy lodged under the front axle.

"Alright," started Brent, "we can use levers or pulleys, but pulleys will take more time to set up and require attachment to our lifting beam up there so let's assume we are using levers."

"I agree," said Abby, "although I would love to weld up a cool lifting frame. There are a bunch of 4x4 blocks behind the shop. Let's get all those for cribbing and I will go look for the strongest and longest beam for lifting in the metal racks."

Within a few minutes, the group was carrying all the 4x4s to a pile next to the truck and Griffin was laying down and starting to stack a few rows of cribbing under the frame. About the time he had the blocks stacked to the frame, Abby staggered out from the storage room with a large 3-inch (75 mm) diameter square steel post that was about 8 feet (2.4m) long.

"Are you ready Griff?" asked Abby.

"Yep, right here," as he placed the post between the top 2 blocks. "We probably need 2-3 people to lift."

Cable, Brent, and Abby pressed down on the lever the truck lifted just enough for Griffin to add the next 2 blocks.

"Alright, move to the next level," instructed Griffin.

With another push, the truck inched up enough for the next layer of blocks. "Are we high enough," asked Brent.

"One more level, I think," said Griffin.

Sure enough, with one more level, the truck was high enough that Griffin was able to extricate the dummy from under the axle.

"14 minutes flat," exclaimed Cody to Mr. Alpin who was sitting nearby.

"Speaking of flat, glad you got the dummy out in time. You earned an early release, but I will be in the lab at lunch in case you need to come by to work on the project," said Mr. Alpin.

An hour later, as lunch began, a few students filed in, some carrying their lunch and sat down at the work tables. Food is not allowed in the lab, but the teachers did not want to discourage lunchtime collaboration and fun, so they informally agreed to allow food at the first couple of tables while work is done at the others. Cody had his laptop open, Mia had her book open. Maggie, Quorra, and Carly entered, carrying their lunches and chatting.

Cable entered the room, clutching his large Nalgene with his typical smile on his face.

"Cable, why does that new girl, Bekah, look familiar?" asked Mr. Alpin.

"That's Bekah Milano, the actress. She was just in that action movie with her dad," replied Cable.

"Oh, right. It was so out of context to have her in the class."

"Mr. Alpin, if you worked for NASA doing all sorts of cool projects, why did you leave to become a teacher? Did you make the Mars mission crash or something?"

One never knows what young engineering minds will think of, nor do you know what they will ask. Mr. Alpin looked up, Maggie and Quorra stopped talking, and even Cody stopped typing. Cable got right to the point and asked what others think but are too shy to ask openly. "You have been telling us that engineering is the highest paid profession with just a BS degree and you seem to enjoy it. Why would you leave it and the money to come teach?"

Brent, Griffin, and Jackson entered the lab and noted the lack of normal chatter and clatter of keys and just sat down. "Valid question," started Mr. Alpin.

"What was the question?" blurted Brent.

"Why did I leave engineering to become a teacher?" Mr. Alpin paused, "How many of you want to impact the world? To save lives? To make a difference?"

Several students nodded, somewhat shocked that Cable had dared to enter a teacher's private life.

"As a surgeon, how many lives can you save per year? Let's do the math. Assume 52 weekends and holidays so about 250 work days per year max and 1-2 surgeries per day so that's about 350-400 people per year if you did surgery every day with no other appointments. Depending on what you do, those are either fixing somebody's parts or saving lives or some combination. As an engineer, if you develop a water filter for developing nations that costs less than $3, how many millions of people will not die from contaminated water per year? As a matter of fact, I just heard about some engineers at P&G who were working on finding a way to remove dirt from laundry water and found a way to purify nasty water with all kinds of parasites and bacteria and now make purifier packets at a loss. Sometimes it is not about the money; it's just the right  thing to do. Do you realize when you enable a community to have clean drinking water that not only does it cure the obvious disease issues, but it also reduces the need to burn fuels to boil water, reduces the time to prepare food, and many other improvements for the community?"

Mr. Alpin continued, "I worked on a generator system that was being developed to go into remote villages in Africa and it was eliminating the way the warlords maintained power over the people, because they did not control the distributed generation of power."

"Or Cody, if you develop software that automates cars in traffic, how many accidents will you prevent? Also, right now, they are developing a fluid in Sweden that is able to absorb the energy from the sun and then it can store that heat energy for over a decade and then release that heat when the fluid is passed through a catalyst."

"Can you imagine what you can do with that? I was able to do some fun work putting things in space and generating electricity from dairy farm digester gasses, but my next mission is to inspire you to be engineers. Just as one invention can impact millions, how much more can I do with a few inventors, each who can create their own inventions? So, my goal is to change the world instead of just inventing things."

"But the money?" asked Mia.

"Yeah, what money?" joked Mr. Alpin. "My mother died while in her mid-50s. Since then I have lived with a different mission. I try to live each day like it really matters, not just to fill a desk and bring home a paycheck. I am not content to just make one impact per day and check off a box. I want to keep making impacts all day until I am forced to sleep. I measure life differently now. I measure it in lives, your lives. I want to not put off any goals or dreams but do it now. Live boldly, every day. If there is a worthwhile goal or dream that fits with my overall plan, I set my sights and do not stop until I accomplish my goal or modify my plan. It's hard to explain and I am sure I irritate many people with my determination, but I move forward every day. The short answer to your questions is simply that I am here to inspire you. The word 'inspire' is from the word 'spirit' so literally I am trying to put spirit into you, breathe motivation, dreams, ideas, and desire into you to be innovators. Live boldly."

"Whoa," said Cable. "That was way more answer than I was expecting. Sorry if it was too personal. You should write a book."

Conversations continued at each table. Cable, Griffin, and Brent ended up at one table.

"Do you think we could actually be engineers?" asked Griffin quietly to his two friends.

"I haven't really been sure that I could handle the classes," said Cable.

"But Mr. Alpin keeps talking like we are already engineers and I am starting to believe it," said Griffin with a growing smile. "I have just been tinkering on my racecar but not really thinking that I could be an engineer like Maggie getting the perfect grades or wonder-Freshman Mia who took physics before me."

"I have to run to class."

"Me too. See you later."

CHAPTER 10 – TIME TO ROLL

Software innovation, like almost every other kind of innovation, requires the ability to collaborate and share ideas with other people, and to sit down and talk with customers and get their feedback and understand their needs. - Bill Gates

Griffin entered the class and launched into conversation, "Mr. Alpin, I was working with gun powder over the weekend and–"

"Wait, what?" said Mr. Alpin. "Am I going to have to report this if you tell me more?"

"No, no. I don't think so. Anyway, I was working with gun powder and I was helping my uncle reload shells, but I took some and put it inside a small container and–"

"You probably shouldn't tell me any more. Well, maybe at lunchtime," said Mr. Alpin. "And be careful, OK? Griffin, this will be right up your alley. We are going to put everything we have learned into one last topic before we leave. Let's make it moooove. Let's start with batteries and add motors and wheels on this and get rolling. It won't be a Tesla, but it will have all the basics."

"Are we making a car?" sizzled Griffin.

"We are transforming stored electrical energy into kinetic energy or motion," answered Mr. Alpin. "The gunpowder you were telling me about is an example of stored energy, stored chemical energy. In the case of electricity, we will start with a battery. How do we get from a battery to motion with what we know?"

"If we make a coil and flow current, we can make a field, but that only causes one linear movement like a solenoid," said Bekah, the class looking at her in disbelief.

"We should just get this out in the open sooner rather than later," started Bekah. "Yes, I am an actress, mostly because my dad is in the business and it's fun. Since I have been home-schooled or tutored on-set I have been able to study physics and engineering and I like it, so I wanted to come here to study with a class when I can fit it in my schedule. There, can we get back to motors?"

"You go girl," said Abby.

"Welcome to engineering class," said Cable as Maggie eyed him.

Impressed with her bold nature, Mr. Alpin said, "Alright, glad we worked that out. What if we could have 3 windings and orient them around a center axis. Each one would have a north and south pole and then we had permanent magnets attached to a rotor. Then we switched the current between those windings so that the north pole keeps pulling to the next south pole, chasing the pulse around in circles. We could have the magnets stationary and put the windings on the rotor and the rotation itself will create the switching or commutation for the windings. What have we just described?"

"Brush motors," said Griffin enthusiastically.

"Yes," said Mr. Alpin. "The brush motors are simple and easy to make but have slightly lower efficiency and shorter life because of brush wear. The advantage is that all you need is a source of current, like a battery, and you get motion, no electronics needed. We are not done yet. We must get that motion changed to higher torque and lower speed and then transmit that to the ground. What's next?"

"We can use a transmission, maybe just a chain and sprockets or some gears. Gears push each other apart and require precision bearings and spacing. Chains and sprockets pull towards each other and are forgiving about spacing. We used them in the robotics club I was in," said Brent. "We can get chain and sprockets off of a bike or motorcycle and then we just need wheels."

"What are the next questions you need to ask to specify the gearing and tires?" asked Mr. Alpin.

"What are the loads and the terrain?" asked Maggie.

"Yes, you are defining the requirements."

"If we have low loads and flat ground, we can use high gears to go fast and if we have higher loads or uneven terrain, we should use low gears or more gear ratio to get the torque," said Abby.

"How about the tires?" asked Mr. Alpin.

"Smooth and low rotational inertia for speed on flat ground and knobby for traction on rough terrain," answered Griffin.

"You have just designed an electric vehicle," affirmed Mr. Alpin as he smiled. "Now let's build it as a go-kart, so we can finish by the end of the week. There is a box of electric motors in the supply room."

The growing confidence was evident as the students plunged right in to get motors and started planning. They asked the right questions to identify the requirements and stayed on task.

"Mr. Alpin, can we ask you a question?" asked Cable as they worked.

"Sure, what's up?" asked Mr. Alpin.

"We know you go to church and you are an engineer and scientist. How do you deal with the conflict?" asked Cable.

"What conflict?" asked Mr. Alpin.

"Can you be a person of science and believe in God?"

"Valid question," said Mr. Alpin. "Not related to electric vehicles but interesting. Let's use the tools we have learned. What is the problem we want to solve? Is there really a conflict between religion and science? Is that about it?"

"Yes," said Mia.

"So, I have engineered hardware to go to Mars, Saturn, and drill into a comet. The one problem we had in every case is that we didn't know the exact environment that we had to design for. We sort of knew the temperature but not the surface texture, rock hardness, sand grain size or soil-to-rock ratio and how conditions were going to change over time. As an engineer, I am tasked with designing for the environment but not overdesign. The ideal design would be something that would modify over time to adapt to its environment. Wouldn't you agree?"

"Yes," said Bekah, as she leaned in.

"I believe that God is the ultimate engineer and has designed organisms to adapt. That requires the design of each organism to have a semi-random set of rules that allow for individual offspring variability but stay similar to its inherited history. Each generation's environment would select the strongest specimens over time so that the species would survive. I would make the case that genetics is the best divine design for a species and universe to survive. Science and God are not just intertwined, science is the study of how God designed the universe. All those laws we study in physics are just the building blocks or rules that God uses in a consistent way to create the Universe."

"Interesting," said Jackson, surprised to get such a detailed answer.

"Ready to make an electric vehicle?" asked Mr. Alpin.

"Yep, we have motors and materials for a chassis," said Abby.

"I have a battery and a cortex ready to program," said Cody.

"I found some wheels in storage," Griffin added.

"We have enough time to get the chassis designed, but we will mount the motors and figure out the transmission in the next couple of days," said Cody.

"You are on a roll!" said Mr. Alpin.

The class groaned faintly as they exited the lab.

CHAPTER 11 – ROLLING

Imagination is not only the uniquely human capacity to envision that which is not, and therefore the fount of all invention and innovation. In its arguably most transformative and revelatory capacity, it is the power that enables us to empathize with humans whose experiences we have never shared. - J. K. Rowling

Griffin had been coming into the lab after school and during lunch to work on the go-kart. Mr. Alpin's primary task was just keeping him safe and focused. Other students had been dropping by to work on various parts, but Griffin and Abby were an unstoppable force of welding and assembly. Cable had been true to his name and been working on wiring, the batteries, and getting the motor installed. No one was quite sure what Cable's real name was, he had been called Cable since middle school and it fit with his skills in hardware, software, and electrical. The steering had not been worked out yet and time was running short.

"What is the status on the electric vehicle?" asked Mr. Alpin as students entered the lab.

"We have a chassis, 36-volt brush motor connected to rear wheels, brakes, a seat, and batteries but the steering and front wheels are giving us some trouble," said Griffin.

"Alright, let's get that worked out today," said Mr. Alpin. "What wheels do you have for the front?"

"We have some bearing-mounted wheels, casters, and some fixed wheels that have their own mounting brackets," answered Cable.

Not waiting until everyone arrived, Mr. Alpin continued, "What is the issue with turning?"

"It is complicated to do a rack and pinion design," said Griffin.

"What is the problem we need to solve?" asked Mr. Alpin.

"We need to steer the vehicle," answered Maggie.

"Right. How many ways are there to do that? Remember, we need to pull back from the problem and look at all the ways to turn a vehicle. Think of all vehicles and their steering. Just name some vehicles that have different steering."

"Tricycle, only 1 wheel turns to steer."

"That makes it easy," started Mr. Alpin, "but what are the problems?

"It is not stable during the turn," answered Bekah.

"Thrusters?" offered Brent.

"Those work best in space where you just need force vectors, but I like your thinking. Any other wheeled vehicle steering systems you might remember from your childhood?"

"Wagon," said Mia.

"How does a wagon work?" asked Mr. Alpin.

"Both wheels turn together on a fixed bar," answered Mia.

"Correct. Let's look at the physics of steering for a moment so we can evaluate the options. When an automobile goes around a corner, what do the wheel paths look like?"

"2 tracks, about 2 meters apart," answered Mia.

"Right. If the same car is making 2 tracks that have different radii, what can you say about their arc lengths?" asked Mr. Alpin.

"The outer one is longer," said Jackson.

"Yes. If one is longer, but both were traveled by the same vehicle in the same time, what can you say about the rotational speed of both tires?"

"The outer one had to go faster," said Brent and then paused. "...and that means that they cannot be on the same axle going the same speed."

"Precisely," said Mr. Alpin. "That is why we have differentials in cars, that large pumpkin-looking thing under the car between the rear wheels. It allows the wheels to be driven by one driveshaft, but one can spin faster to go around curves. Will the wagon method work for our vehicle?'

"As long as they are not on one driveshaft," began Shelbi. "We could use 2 of the simple fixed caster wheels since they each have their own axle and bracket."

"Any other steering systems?" asked Mr. Alpin. "So far, we have 1-wheel tricycle, 2-wheel wagon, and 2-wheel car?"

"We could use omni wheels and drive the rear wheels independently with different speeds," said Cody.

"True," said Mr. Alpin. "A great example of how a software engineer can solve a mechanical problem. How does car steering work, by the way?

Griffin was laying on his back and assembling while this discussion was taking place, but he chimed in, "The 2 wheels are mounted on pivots, but they are connected via a parallelogram such that the 2 wheels move parallel to each other while steering. The parallelogram is shifted from side to side with a Pitman arm and idler arm that is driven by the steering system. I just connected mine in my car a few weeks ago."

"How many mounting points and pivots are in a car steering system?" asked Mr. Alpin.

"There are the wheels that pivot top and bottom, so that is 4. Then there are the parallelogram parts which are another 3, 4, 5, 6 or so places," answered Griffin.

"That sounds complicated," said Jackson. "Can we just do the wagon?"

"What are the pros and cons?" asked Mr. Alpin.

"I suppose for small angles it is about the same," said Cable. "When steering at high angles the wheels will not provide the same wide footprint when the steering bar turns."

"Great observation," said Mr. Alpin. "So, what meets the requirements?"

"Since we are not trying to be street-legal or going high performance, I think we can use the wagon steering," said Brent.

"Do you have the materials you need? Have you run the calcs to know what you can use?" asked Mr. Alpin.

"If we are supporting 200 pounds, divided by 4 wheels but assuming dynamic loading due to steering we figure we should use wheels that are rated for at least 250 and better if they are 500 pounds," said Maggie.

"I agree," said Mr. Alpin. "You realize that bearing performance is a matter of lifetime. You can use many different bearings, but they will yield different life expectancy. You could use a metal shaft in a hole in a wood block if you turn slowly enough with low load and not need a long life, but if you want 100,000-mile performance like in a car, you need to do the calcs and make sure your L10 life is enough to meet the needs."

"L10 life[vi]?" asked Maggie.

"Sorry, that will be something you don't cover until later or at university. It is the life calculation for bearings assuming 90% reliability and takes into a lot of factors like speed, temperature, lubrication, axial load, thrust load. You need to pick a wheel that has a rated load that will handle your expected loads and life."

"We will use these since they are rated for 200 kg, have tread, are bearing mounted, and are $17," proposed Abby.

"Perfect. Notice that the side brackets are slightly curved? What does that do for us?" asked Mr. Alpin.

"The curve increases the bending strength, so they won't parallelogram," said Brent.

"What do you mean?" checked Mr. Alpin.

"If the brackets are flat, they will bend and the wheel will tip."

"Well done. I will order them. Get to work."

Everyone gathered around and was pitching in. Final touches were getting installed and then Mr. Alpin came around the corner with 2 wheels. "These are close. Will they work for the prototype?" asked Mr. Alpin.

"Sure, and we can swap them out after the conference. Let's do this. Thanks," said Griffin.

Within minutes the wheels were installed on the steering bar and it was getting mounted on the chassis. After flipping the cart over Griffin grabbed the old steering wheel from his race car and screwed it in place.

"Is the electrical done, Cable?" asked Griffin.

"Yep, just need to install the fuse."

"Who's taking the first ride?" asked Mr. Alpin.

"Maggie, you ought to take the first ride," said Griffin. "You made all our calculations come out to make sure it would work."

"But, I only...." Maggie dipped her face down.

"You are amazing, and we could not have done it without you," said Cable as the group nodded in agreement.

"Remember what Mr. Alpin said about writing your own story," said Shelbi.

"What about you?" asked Cable.

"I'm still writing mine," said Shelbi.

"Aren't we all still writing our stories? So am I," said Mr. Alpin. "I can already see how Shelbi is more confident, Maggie is finding her inner leader, Brent is being a better listener, and you all are becoming engineers. I'm so proud of you. OK. Hop in Maggie."

Maggie looked down and then back up and smiled. "OK." She stepped into the cart and placed her hands on the wheel, clicked on the power and pressed on the throttle. She sailed out into the parking lot, silently and swiftly, then let out a holler, "wooo whooooo!"

Once you have an innovation culture, even those who are not scientists or engineers - poets, actors, journalists - they, as communities, embrace the meaning of what it is to be scientifically literate. They embrace the concept of an innovation culture. They vote in ways that promote it. They don't fight science and they don't fight technology. - Neil deGrasse Tyson

The students gathered at the last class meeting before their flight.

"I fly out tonight, so I just wanted to review before I leave," said Mr. Alpin. "I see you have everything packed and sitting by the door of the lab. That's great, now let's talk about your presentation. Remember, this is just like all the design reviews you have been doing for years, except with more people watching. You explain..."

"What are the requirements," finished Griffin.

"What we did, what we assumed, and why we did what we did," added Maggie.

"Wow, you have been listening," joked Mr. Alpin. "Seriously, though. I am proud of you all and know that you will do great. You have developed your skills so well this year. I want to reflect on how you are all writing your new life story, so for class today you need to write a paragraph about who you were when you came into the first day of school 9 months ago, then another paragraph about who you are now, and a third paragraph about who you want to be next. Remember, the next page is blank. You can invent the new you and it is only fear and memories that hold you back."

"What about bad grades?" asked Cable.

"They might delay you or require that you take a class again or go to community college for a while, but you can overcome that and be the engineer or accountant or doctor or scientist or teacher that you want to be. You also might need to change friend groups or change habits to have a different life. Don't expect that you can keep doing the same thing and get different results. OK, write your stories in the next 10-15 minutes. You don't have to share, so just be honest with yourself."

Mr. Alpin sat down at one of the desks as the class scribbled away. He was doing the same assignment. This was his first year teaching and was writing new chapters in his life and felt this was the perfect time to reflect with everyone else.

Some students stared out the window as they thought, and some started tapping on their laptops right away. Mr. Alpin had been an engineer, owned his own business then became a teacher. Each change had been intimidating, filled with unknowns, but each change was easier than the first, practice builds confidence. Mr. Alpin looked up at the class and noticed that Mia was wiping her eyes. Cody was still not writing and had his eyes closed.

Mr. Alpin said softly to the whole class, "I realize that this exercise can be difficult for some as it may open up a painful past, so maybe your next page could be as simple as letting go of an experience or relationship."

After several minutes, Mr. Alpin walked around the room as the students were finishing. As he passed through the class, he patted

Mia on the shoulder, letting her know she wasn't alone with her feelings and emotions.

"Alright, I hope this has been helpful. Let's go over our final lists and get ready. Those who are not going to the conference are welcome to study or read on your own."

After 15 minutes of checking boxes of equipment, presentation materials and making final copies of their PowerPoint presentations in various formats to ensure they would work, Mr. Alpin closed with, "See you in Prague."

CHAPTER 13 – FLIGHT

For once you have tasted flight you will walk the earth with your eyes turned skywards, for there you have been and there you will long to return. - Leonardo da Vinci

The engineering conference items had been safely packed into the Pelican shipping containers, the students were gathered with their bags at school at 4 p.m., ready to get on the vans to the airport. The big day had finally come.

"Has anyone studied where we are actually going?" asked Griffin.

"I downloaded some pages about Prague and bought the Lonely Planet guide for the area, but I don't know how much time we will have to explore. Our close connection in Frankfort will keep us on our toes and we have to go directly to the university from the airport," said Maggie.

4:07 p.m. Dean Slothour rounded the corner and methodically scanned the group and asked, "Are all 8 of you here? I have your tickets; the flight is at 10 p.m. out of Bradley Terminal. Do you each have your permission forms? Phone chargers and adapters? Jackets?" The irony of his questions with lack of replies was not lost on the group, it's not like they could go get any of the missing items now, but they were ready. "It's cold since you will be at the 50th parallel, more north than the northern border of the US with Canada.

Mr. Alpin is already in Prague for the meetings before the presentations. I will get you to the airport and he will meet you tomorrow. Put your backpacks and bags in the back and get in the van."

Only some of the students had traveled before and were offering advice to their classmates. Shelbi was biting her nails while looking at her phone and Mia was reading, like usual. Abby was looking at her phone, but more like she was looking through it to some far point in the distance. Cody was on his laptop, making final adjustments for their project. Griffin was asleep. Brent was listening to everything and Maggie was reading her Lonely Planet guide, occasionally reading a sentence aloud to the group.

The flight was basically filled with much of the same, watching lots of movies on the streaming seat-back displays. The excitement of the trip made it impossible for anyone to sleep much, except for Griffin who was not used to confinement with lack of things to do.

A dawn landing in Frankfort jolted the group with nervous energy from a restless night. During a quick run through the airport to make the connecting flight, Shelbi managed to buy 3 dark Toblerone chocolates and 2 others got Starbucks and made it to the distant gate. The gate was in the part of the airport where only the small planes board. As they arrived at the gate there was some confusion at the desk with lots of discussion in German. Maggie approached the desk first and said that they were checking in as a group of 8 for the flight. The gate attendant pivoted away from the conversation behind the counter and asked, "Are you ze group from ze flight from Los Angeles?"

"Yes, that's us."

"Are you all here?"

"All except two who are coming from the restroom now."

"OK. We had some electrical issues and have moved ze other passengers to an earlier flight thinking your group might not make it. Ze plane has just been cleared and we are getting it ready. Have a seat and we will board you soon."

"How many seats are on this plane?" asked Cody.

"This ATR-42 has 48 seats, so it will be your group of 8 and 2 others if they show up."

"48," said Brent as he turned around to look out the window to see a small turboprop sitting on the ramp. "Well, it will probably be a bumpy ride, but at least with a turboprop, they can glide better and stop faster on short runways."

A few minutes later, a nicely dressed couple arrived at the gate and were promptly boarded on the plane. The gate attendant did not need to use a microphone in this quiet end of the airport but instead motioned to the group and she scanned their tickets, closed the gate with a retractable strap and followed the group down the stairs and across the wet pavement to the pull-down stairs of the plane. Each engineering student was evaluating the small plane as they carried their backpacks and shielded their faces from the heavy mist. Griffin noted that the luggage and 2 white Pelican cases were on a cart next to the plane. As they boarded, they passed the couple who were sipping champagne in a row in front of a curtain. The woman appeared to sneer as each student passed the curtain and flopped into their own pair of seats, starting at the rear. Griffin bumped his head a few times as he maneuvered his 6'4" frame into a seat near the front of the group, still several rows behind the curtain.

The flight attendant, the same woman from the gate, stood up at the front of the plane and gave the safety briefing, no fancy animated or computer-generated instructional video like the one on the 777.

The plane taxied out to the runway and appeared to be a toy compared to the jets on the taxiway. The loud fan noise of the turboprops made conversation difficult, so each student mostly looked out their rain-streaked windows. Dark forest passed below, dotted with an occasional farm and field. Villages were small and infrequent as they bumped their way toward Prague. The students plugged in their music and closed their eyes.

About 45 minutes into their hour and a half flight the plane began to shake as it encountered stormy weather over the mountains. The flight attendant was bustling about and storing things. Lightning flashed outside the windows.

"This is like the dark cloudy sky and the compression zone we saw on our retreat trip in the Sierras," said Brent. "Griff, doesn't it seem like we are flying lower than normal? If we are halfway through an hour and a half flight, we should be at cruising altitude, but we seem to be just skimming the trees." Their faces grew pale and sweaty palms gripped the armrests. Shelbi pulled the earbuds from her ears.

Lightning flashed and the plane shuttered. The engine sound changed, slightly slower as the plane descended a bit more, then the engines went quiet, replaced by an eerie swishing sound. The students looked at each other in alarm.

"Prepare for a water landing! Crash positions!" was the only call over the speakers. The attendant pulled the curtain back and in a shaky but firm voice said, "Put your seatbelts on, fold your arms over your head, brace for impact and prepare for a water landing. Remember, your floatation devices are under your seats."

CHAPTER 14 — LANDING

Without tradition, art is a flock of sheep without a shepherd. Without innovation, it is a corpse. - Winston Churchill

Looking out the windows they could see nothing but forest close below them and a dark, cloudy sky above and then it opened up with water on their left and land on their right, except that the land was a steep mountain that rose from the water. The silence slowed time as their minds were processing all the data. Ahead and to the right was what appeared to be a Ferris wheel. The plane did glide well, but the pilot did not have much to choose from for landing locations. Just as it seemed the plane would touch down on the water, they put their heads down, and the plane touched down roughly. They violently shook as the plane bounced and suddenly there was a crash and a terrifying ripping of metal that sounded like an explosion without fire and the cabin was filled with cold air as the plane lurched. Things went flying through the cabin as terror exploded in their ears. Everything stopped moving. Their hearts felt like they were trying to keep the plane aloft on their own. Silence.

"Is everyone ok?" called Griffin.

The cabin lights were out, but there was light coming from the front. There were some muffled replies about the time that Griffin stood and looked back as the light reflected off the pale faces of his classmates. He turned to look forward and the front section of the plane was missing, just the rough edge of fuselage, insulation, and wiring hung from the end of the cabin a couple of rows in front of where he was sitting. "Oh my God. Where did it go?" he whispered. The cockpit, flight attendant, and the couple in first class were gone.

Griffin started making his way back through the plane over bags and debris in the aisle and checking on each person and soon the group was together at the front edge of the open fuselage. Several were bruised and blood trickled from Brent's forehead. There was no smell of fuel or smoke.

"Wait! Where is Mia!" Griffin shouted.

"She was sitting behind me," said Brent.

Griffin leaped over seats like they were hurdles and looked in the row behind where Brent had been sitting. She was crumpled on the floor with blood on her arm and head. He shook her shoulder and grasped her small arm where it was bleeding. "Mia, are you OK?"

She moaned and lifted her head. "Ya."

"Does anything hurt?"

"Not really, except my arm and you've got that."

Seeing that her head and neck were still working, he picked her up and moved her to the front opening of the fuselage. Shelbi propped herself against an armrest, she was missing her crutch, it was in some compartment. Looking around her, she spied an airline blanket and pillow that was hanging from an open compartment. "Hand me those," she directed. Deftly she pulled the pillowcase off and wrapped it around Mia's arm. "Put this pillow under her head and let's cover her in case she goes into shock."

It was still morning, so the air was crisp, and the dew was hanging on the grass near the plane. The lake lapped at the shore nearby to the north and the large skeleton of a Ferris wheel creaked in the morning breeze to the south with a mountain rising steeply behind.

Brent and Cody limped a bit to see the forward section of the plane. The cockpit had taken the brunt of the impact and was hardly recognizable, but just as they stood there in disbelief, they heard a faint moan. The woman from first class was still strapped into a seat but it was laying on its side in the wet dirt. As they rushed to her they could see her husband had been less fortunate as most of his body was still in the forward section of the plane.

They kept her in the seat and rotated it upright to check for injuries. Shelbi instructed Abby to hold the wrapping around Mia's arm. Griffin found her crutch and helped Shelbi down from the torn fuselage. She hobbled over to the woman. While Griffin and Cody got everyone lowered to the ground, Shelbi was checking vital signs and inspecting the woman's head and neck. "I am trained in First Aid and CPR. Can I help you?" she asked.

"Yes," the woman said weakly. "Where is my ... Where is the man I was with?"

The group was silent for that extra moment that says what does not need to be said, and Maggie whispered only, "I'm so sorry."

While Shelbi, Maggie, and Cable were attending to the woman, Cody and Griffin stood together looking at the scene around them. "Where? Where are the people?" asked Cody, shock in his voice. "A plane just crashed next to an amusement park and there is no one around."

"It's abandoned," said Cable.

"We are alone," said Griffin, just loud enough that the rest of the group all turned to look at him. Then, quieter for only Cody to hear, "It happened so fast I doubt the pilot got a call out. There was no fireball for people to see. I haven't seen a town for a while, only the occasional road. We are on our own."

They started to take inventory of the scene around them. It appeared that they were on a road along the shore of a lake in front of an abandoned amusement park with a Ferris wheel, roller coasters, and other attractions. Seeing the rust and growth of the trees and foliage it had been years since it was occupied. Brent took a couple of pictures.

vii

"We need a plan," said Griffin.

'We need help, my phone has no signal," said Maggie.

"We need to build a shelter," added Brent.

CHAPTER 15 – ASSESSMENT

Without change, there is no innovation, creativity, or incentive for improvement. Those who initiate change will have a better opportunity to manage the change that is inevitable. - William Pollard

Most of the group had moved up away from the plane and were sitting along a boardwalk on some benches that were shedding faded paint flakes.

"It's just before 9 a.m. There are 8 of us and the woman from the plane. Where did she go, by the way? Oh, she's sitting by the plane with Shelbi. I'll go get them." said Maggie.

They surveyed the scene around them. It appeared that the plane hit a dock or wall that pivoted the plane into a concrete abutment that sheared the front end off but did not damage the wings or fuel tanks.

"The cockpit is messed up," started Griffin. "It looks like one of those car accidents that is so bad you can't tell what type or color the car used to be."

"The high-wing design probably helped keep the rest of the plane from getting tangled up in the mess," said Cable.

Brent added, "This amusement park is located on the shore of a lake and is surrounded by mountains. I don't see anyone."

"The crew is gone," whispered Mia. "The crew is gone. We are alone and no one knows where we are. There is no one to take care of us, like before," she trailed off. A tear ran down her face and she closed her eyes.

The group sat in silence as the water lapped at the shore and the breeze flapped the insulation at the edge of the plane.

"OK," said Cable. "We can do this. Let's sit for a bit and think. I bet we can find something here we can use."

"There's got to be equipment, tools, vehicles, and other stuff in this park, right?" asked Griffin.

Cody turned on his phone, waited, turned it off, and put his head down. "Has anyone else tried their phone and what are the options for charging? Mine had no service, surprise, surprise."

"I have no service, but I have a solar charger," said Cable.

"We should have lots of daylight left today," said Abby.

"There is some weather on the ridges, so we should make sure we have shelter before that happens. The cargo hold is in the rear of the plane and maybe we can get some of our clothes," said Brent.

"How about if we team up and take care of things?" asked Abby.

"What are the problems we need to solve?" asked Maggie. "For the first 24 hours, we need shelter, clothes, water, list of resources, map, anything else?"

Maggie was just bringing the woman to the group, "This is Sterling. She appears to be bruised and her legs are banged up, but nothing broken."

Cable proposed, "How about Griffin and I look in the park. Abby and Brent check out the cargo. Shelbi and Mia stay with Sterling. Cody and Maggie look for shelter. Anything else? Let's meet back here in about an hour."

"OK, let's go."

Abby and Brent made their way back to the plane but made it a point to avoid the deadly scene of the forward section. The cargo door was still secure, and it was not obvious how to open it without a tool. They worked their way to the end that was ripped away. They noticed that the space under the floor was also exposed although covered in dangling wires and shreds of carpet, plastic, and aluminum.

"I think I am seeing into the hold," said Abby.

"I can probably fit in there," said Brent.

"Be careful of the sharp edges. Here is a blanket to lay over that."

"I see the Pelican cases and there are other bags back in here. Let me push them out to you. Luckily, we packed light with backpacks, and they are fitting but I don't think the Pelicans or these two large black cases will make it out," said Brent, grunting as he pushed things around.

After making several trips and pushing the small bags through the mess of wires and insulation, Brent said, "I am coming out now, but will leave the big ones."

"Let's look in the kitchen area for any food or water," said Brent as he climbed into the upper part of the plane where the seats are. "You can stay down there; I'll be back in a minute."

He was gone a few minutes and returned with 3 cases of bottled water and a box.

"There isn't much food on this plane, only those bags of pretzel things they served us on the flight," said Brent. "Let me hand these down to you."

Abby added, "I bet they had better snacks and drinks in First Class. I don't think we can even find the forward galley, though."

After stacking the water and pretzels near the luggage, they both looked at the forward section of the plane.

"Let's see what we can find in the cockpit," said Abby.

"Yeah, maybe we can find a radio."

The nose of the plane appeared to have hit the seawall and crushed the cockpit severely. They could not find a way in, or if there was an inside to be found. "I don't see much, oh, I think that is the pilot in there, but he is not ...," Brent trailed off. "I don't think there will be anything working in there, just too mashed. Well, let's take the water and bags back to the group."

Looking like a busy mother who is trying to carry too many shopping bags back from the minivan, they slung bags and backpacks around their necks and arms and waddled back to the group with the first load.

Cody and Maggie headed for the buildings near the center of the park.

"Let's find a place to sleep or hide from rain. And not there," said Cody as he pointed to a tattered old building that read 'Cool Zone'.

There was a roller coaster in the background and plants growing over every building. Most doors were locked but they did find a few that were open.

"You know what this graffiti means?" asked Cody.

"I don't recognize the words," replied Maggie.

"No, it means someone has been here which means there is a way here and a way out."

"Good point," replied Maggie. "What's in that building?"

Cody ran in and exited a few minutes later while Maggie checked some other doors.

"That is a kitchen," said Cody. "If we only had food. Let's look out back if they have propane."

"There are two white tanks, but not sure what they are since the markings are in some language I don't read."

"Let me turn on the valves out here and you go in and see if you can turn something on," said Cody.

Cody traced the pipes and turned on the tank valve, then the building valve and heard Maggie yell from inside so he shut down the tank valve. "The stove was hissing when I turned it on," said Maggie.

"Great, we have heat and cooking," said Cody.

They worked their way from ticket buildings, a small theater, a game arcade, to supply buildings that were locked up and they found a smaller building behind the others. They peered through dusty windows and wiped them to see bunks inside. "This looks like staff quarters," said Maggie.

Cody found a pipe that was a couple meters long and wedged it between the door lever and the frame and pulled. After creaking a bit, there was a pop and the door lever dropped to the floor.

Reaching into the door lock mechanism with a stick he pulled to the left and the door opened. They had found staff quarters, about a dozen bunks and bathrooms, but no water was flowing.

"This looks good for sleeping but it is a long way from the kitchen, water, and other stuff. How about we circle back that direction and see what we find," said Maggie.

The brush had grown up around the buildings and through every crack in the pavement so what used to be obvious roads and paths were just suggestions of where to walk. It required carefully picking through the plants and watching for cast-off materials that littered the grounds. There were pipes and frames, lumber, hoses, and old tires.

They could see through the bars and a dirty window of an old maintenance shed, lawnmowers and tools, but it was latched shut. As they made their way closer to the public part of the park, they found more locked buildings, some with broken windows. One building was large with metal siding and a roll-up door at one end and several higher windows along the side.

"I think I can get into this one if you give me a boost through that window," said Cody.

He rolled a wheel over to the window and then reached up while Maggie gave him a boost. "This is a warehouse," he called from inside. "Just a bunch of boxes, trash, and pallets of more boxes. I am going to see what's inside these boxes."

"Cleaning supplies," he called. "Hydraulic oil, cases of oil." A minute later, "T-shirts! We can have souvenirs." "Bags of something heavy, just a sec. Rice! I guess it was cheaper to leave it than move it. I'm going to keep looking." Several minutes later, he held up cans of *fazole, broskve, mixovaná zelenina,* and *kukuřice.* "There are other cans, but I can't read any of them."

Suddenly, Cody rolled open the door from the inside and stood holding a bag of rice.

Cable and Griffin were running from building to shed looking for vehicles, supplies, or anything else they could find. The park was large, and they had the same obstacle field that Maggie and Cody were dealing with, but they weren't trying to break into buildings, more getting a survey of the park.

"The creepiest thing is how things are just left how they were when the park closed," said Cable.

Moving like squirrels looking for nuts, the two young men ran and jumped over things and yelled out to announce their latest discoveries.

"Bicycles with flat tires!"

"Fire extinguishers!"

"Creepy clown!"

"Rope!"

"Dollies!"

"Stop playing with your dolls, again Griff," joked Cable, trying to make him laugh.

"No, dollies for moving stuff," smiled Griffin as they ran.

"Motorcycle with no front wheel!"

"Check out that carousel!"

"And that water ride."

"Water ride?" Griffin said slowly. "Are there boats?"

"No, just those fiberglass log things," said Cable.

"Are you thinking what I'm thinking?" asked Griffin.

"Unless you are thinking about having some lunch, then probably not," joked Cable.

"How many log boats are there?"

"I just saw about 8 behind that building."

"Alright, let's keep looking."

"Griff! Look! A van."

"That is a UAZ, made in Russia. Their nickname is 'loaf of bread'. I would have preferred a Defender but let's see what we have here. These are amazing for their durability and offroad capability and came in lots of versions, all pretty similar to their original release in the 1960s. They are pretty gutless with only 70-80 horsepower but they can run on pretty low power fuels. Let's see if it is diesel or gas. Most are gas."

"How do you know this stuff?"

"Same way you know computers. I look stuff up. I was researching alternative fuel engines and found some articles on using 72-76 octane gas in the UAZ, but we don't have that garbage in the US, but if it is diesel it can run on other stuff. Gas!" Griffin exclaimed as he found the fuel door. "Who knows if it runs or even has an engine, let alone if there is fuel somewhere."

"Let's go back to the group since our hour is about up."

CHAPTER 16 — INVENTORY

The only way you survive is you continuously transform into something else. It's this idea of continuous transformation that makes you an innovation company. - Ginni Rometty

Brent and Abby returned first with the luggage and brought back a large First Aid kit from the plane as well. They were able to collect almost all the luggage that belonged to the group, but it appeared that one was still missing. They had arranged all the bags on what used to be a sidewalk. The planting areas had erupted with plant life and rained down sprouts and vines into every crack of the park.

Shelbi and Mia had been tending to Sterling and it turned out that she had some significant cuts to her legs that they had been treating and wrapping. Mia's arm was cleaned and wrapped with a clean bandage from the First Aid kit.

Next to return were Griffin and Cable, talking a mile a minute as they were brainstorming all sorts of ideas and their conversation continued as they returned.

"The way I see our situation is that we will need a boat to get across the lake and then need a vehicle to drive from there."

"Can we make a boat out of something?"

"What if we put a propeller on the van and used it as a boat," said Cable.

"Did you find a van?" asked Shelbi.

"Yes, but we don't know if it runs, has fuel or even an engine at this point," answered Griffin.

"It looks like you found our bags. I see mine," said Cable.

"We've been watching the sky get darker with clouds, so I hope Maggie and Cody have found shelter."

"There are a lot of buildings, so we could hunker down anywhere, but not in here," said Cable as he showed a photo of the entrance to a roller coaster tunnel. The bright colors of the dragon face suggested at a previous existence of life and excitement, but now the colors looked like bright makeup on a corpse.

Maggie and Cody came around the corner of the nearest building, stepping carefully around some metal frames.

"What did you find?" asked Griffin.

"Lots of things, but it will take a while to figure out the puzzle that we need to solve," said Maggie. "We found a small bunkhouse, but it was a ways away from the main part of the park and the other buildings and the kitchen."

"Kitchen!" exclaimed Shelbi.

The sudden pronouncement of 'kitchen' reminded everyone they had not eaten in a long time and were quite hungry. "What's for lunch?" joked Shelbi.

"We found cans of something with labels we couldn't read in a warehouse building," said Cody.

The wind suddenly blasted down from the mountain above the park and skittered dry leaves along the cracked walkways.

"Let's focus on moving our stuff to shelter before that weather turns wet," said Brent. "Lead on."

Everyone started standing up and picking up their bags. Cable threw Shelbi's over his other shoulder and Brent did the same with Mia's backpack and Sterling's small bag. Her large one was still stuck in the cargo hold. They helped Sterling stand and walk.

"The shortest route is probably up this way," said Maggie as she pointed up toward the right of the park.

They were all seeing the park together for the first time and it was starting to sink in. Their plane had crashed, killed the crew and one passenger and left the group of teenagers responsible to care for a woman. The clouds darkened, and the obscured sun was dropping behind the ridge above the park. The fact that the amusement park had evidence of once being bright, colorful, happy, and full of life but was now rusted, overgrown, and completely still except for the dry leaves created such a creepy contrast that the group walked closer together as they wound their way up the overgrown walkways.

"Over there," pointed Maggie, "is the warehouse with the cans and stuff, but the bunkhouse is up the hill.

"Where was the kitchen?" asked Shelbi.

"Back that way near the carousel," said Maggie as she pointed.

Climbing over some piles of leaves and trash, the group was headed for the last building on the road they had been following. "Here we are. Home sweet home," said Maggie.

Griffin approached the door, slid the door handle that was on the ground off to the side with his foot, and pushed the door open to reveal the bunks and small bathroom.

"You don't expect me to sleep in here on these dirty cots, do you?" asked Sterling, who had appeared more numb or shell-shocked up to this point.

"You are welcome to stay anywhere you like, but this appears to be the best sleeping quarters we can find. I don't see puddles or water stains on the floor, so it looks like the roof is still intact," said Cody, in his matter-of-fact way.

Everyone, including Sterling, knew that she was in no position to try existing on her own, with her injuries and lack of experience, she had just lost her companion and was not accustomed to the rustic life. She moved to the corner bunk and sat down, staring at the floor.

"Let's compare our notes and make a plan," said Maggie. "What did you find?" looking at Griffin and Cable.

The group started dragging bunks to form a circle. Maggie looked over to Sterling to invite her over, but she just laid down and faced the wall.

"Before we talk about making a plan can we talk about making food?" asked Shelbi.

"Right, Maggie, did you also download the translator when you were getting your Lonely Planet guide?"

"Yes, that's right. I forgot. It's on my phone."

"Outstanding! Maggie, maybe you could take someone back to the warehouse with your translator and see if you can read some of those cans and bring back food," suggested Cody. Cable had found his charger and set it in the window sill and connected it to his phone.

"I'll go get cans with Maggie," said Cable. "Griff, go ahead and update the group on our discoveries while we are gone."

He and Maggie put on jackets and headed out the door.

"We found a van, motorcycle, 2 bicycles, and a bunch of general materials like rope, hose, metal and stuff like that," started Griffin. "The van is gas, but we don't know if it runs, but this type of engine can run on low power fuel."

"We found lots of oil drums, but I assumed they were all hydraulic oil for the roller coaster hydraulics," said Cody. "We should go back and check what all the drums are."

"Do we even know what type of transportation we need?" asked Mia.

Griffin paused and then started, "From what we have seen so far I think that there are no roads out of here and we need to find a way across the lake and then drive or walk until we find civilization. This," he paused again, "is going to take some work, some engineering, and some time. We need to be prepared for the long haul."

Sterling rolled over, "What is a 'long haul?'"

The group had forgotten she was in the room and were startled by her voice. Shelbi invited her over and reached over to offer her a hand, "Come on over. We are one group now." As they both hobbled over to the nearest bunk she continued, "We are quite a group, aren't we? Banged up, bruised, on a crutch, but we're alive." As the word 'alive' dropped into the room, Shelbi remembered Sterling's companion just as she heard her softly sob.

To avoid the awkward moment or just to get back on track, Griffin continued, "The long haul is that it will take weeks to design, build, and execute a plan to get 9 of us out. We need to figure out water, food, warmth, as well as constructing our transportation."

"We should divide into teams," stated Brent. "I would like to work on transportation with Griffin."

"We have shelter, but it's far from the food and kitchen," said Abby.

"What's the problem we need to solve," asked Shelbi.

"We need to live efficiently," said Abby. "Maybe we can move the bunks down the hill near the other facilities. Griff, did you see any dollies or carts?"

"Yes, there were a couple of things like that. Abby, would you work with Brent and me on the transportation?"

"Sure."

"It seems like we ought to explore our perimeter and find out what's around us and if there is a way out," said Mia. "I am a cyclist. Maybe we can get the bike tires filled and someone can come with me to make a map first thing in the morning?"

"OK, tomorrow we need to get some dollies," stopping abruptly, Griffin corrected himself. "We need to find a way to move the bunks. We need to see if the van runs, what fuel is available and think about a boat."

"I like to cook and do it a lot since my parents are gone most of the time," said Shelbi. "I will check out the warehouse and kitchen."

"I can help with that or I have been thinking about the boat and want to do the calculations for buoyancy," said Mia. "How much do you think the van weighs?"

Griffin started thinking aloud, "My Subaru is about 3000 and a VW van is about 3500 so I would guess 4000 pounds plus 9 times 125 is just over 5000 pounds for the group."

"That is about 2300 kilograms so..." Mia trailed off as she was making notes and calculations.

"Who are you kids?" asked Sterling, surprised by their methodical efficiency.

"We're engineering students," started Abby. "And between our group and our training to solve these problems, we will figure it out. We have to."

"What university do you go to?" buoyed by the recent information.

"Oh, we're in high school," said Cody. "Anyway, Griff, Abby, we also found a maintenance shed with tools and lawnmowers and stuff. Maybe there is something useful in there, like a bike pump, but it was locked."

The door burst open and Cable exclaimed, "beans, peaches, mixed vegetables, and corn!"

CHAPTER 17 – FIRED UP

I believe that education is all about being excited about something. Seeing passion and enthusiasm helps push an educational message. - Steve Irwin

After a dinner of peaches, the group gathered and chatted in the growing darkness. Light rain started tapping on the metal roof.

"This reminds me of sitting around the campfire on the retreat weekend," said Abby.

"Campfire," said Cable. "I totally forgot. I have that keychain flint and magnesium from Mr. Alpin. Campfire anyone?"

"Yes, but maybe outside, right?" said Abby.

Cable and Abby moved for the door, the others following quickly. The fresh scent of the rain met them at the entrance.

"Sterling, come outside with us for campfire," said Griffin in his usual enthusiastic way that sounds more like an encouraging coach, who does not expect anything but compliance.

She looked over to see his outstretched hand and rolled off the bunk, not quite sure about this outdoor activity.

Cable, Abby, Maggie, and Cody were running around gathering sticks and old lumber. Shelbi went back inside the bunkhouse and emerged with an old book.

"I saw this earlier hoping it was a book to read, but it is in Czech or something, so maybe we could use it as a fire starter."

"But it's a book," pleaded Mia.

"We need to make tough choices," reassured Cable. "As a matter of survival we may need to do things we wouldn't normally do."

On the concrete in front of the bunkhouse under a porch, Cable assembled a log cabin with a bed of tinder in the center with some crumpled paper and rag at the bottom. He began to strike the flint with the sharp edge of the latch mechanism from the door. After many sparkless tries, he adjusted and pressed down and got a shower of sparks into the rag. A few minutes later there was a sparkle and puff and he blew a steady stream of air on the orange spot, but it went out. He pressed the steel into the flint and the rag sparkled again. Quickly he knelt and blew into the orange glow. A flame danced along the edge of the rag and the paper caught and then the small sticks. He looked up at the group and they seemed to sense what he was thinking. They will be OK if they remember their training, plan ahead, and think things out. The fire grew out of the log cabin and everyone added a few more sticks. They had fire. The smoke pushed against the underside of the porch as the rain danced on the top.

Mostly they were quiet, only quick comments as the fire burned bright and warm. After a while warming themselves by the fire, the conversation faded as larger raindrops hit the metal roof over their campfire as it continued to collapse into an orange glow. The wind pulsed, and the group collectively moved inside the dark building.

"There are more blankets in the back closet," said Mia.

"Wear all your layers and jackets," instructed Griffin. "See you in the morning."

The rain pattered and pounded all through the night. A couple of students woke in complete darkness, heard the rain pounding on the metal roof, wanted to turn on a light, but remembered where they were and tried to fall back to sleep. It was not the most restful night, but the group was dry and safe. At first light, they began to stir and realized their hunger. Griffin opened another can of peaches, ate one and went outside.

The rain had stopped but there were puddles, a cold breeze tumbled leaves down the path. Griffin pulled his jacket up to his chin and hurried along the path. He couldn't help himself and had to satisfy his curiosity. He rounded the last corner and saw the van. He tried the passenger door handle, locked. Driver's door, locked. He went to the rear cargo door and it was hanging slightly askew. He pulled, and it opened roughly with a long squeak. Inside the van were some boxes and barricades. He crawled over them to the front to unlock the doors. The engine for this vehicle was located between the front seats under its own doghouse.

He looked in the ignition just to see if he got lucky but there was no key. As he lifted the engine cover, he was going through a mental checklist of what could be an issue and what he would need to do – dead battery, no fuel, no engine. He found the compartment was appropriately full of parts, except the battery tray that is located behind the driver's seat was empty. This might explain why it was left behind. He traced the other major parts and it appeared to be complete. Without the battery, it would be impossible to check the fuel gauges, starter, or anything else. He lowered the doghouse but did not latch it and smiled to himself. A missing battery was actually good news, it explains why it was left here and might indicate a single cause of non-operation. He looked again at the ignition and the wires that ran from the key cylinder down the steering column. Due to the rather industrial design, it simply had a few wires that were zip-tied to another bundle of wires. Now to find a battery.

Lawnmowers. Lawnmowers have batteries and there was a maintenance shed with lawnmowers. As he thought about the possibilities his pace picked up to a jog. *"Where was that shed?"* he thought to himself as he rounded the corner and almost crashed into Cody. Surprised at the appearance of each they both looked up in momentary shock.

"Where've you been?" asked Cody.

"I had to check the van. Where was that lawnmower maintenance shed?"

"Ugh, over by the warehouse. That way."

Griffin said nothing and started jogging. Cody was groggy and less enthusiastic, but curious enough to follow.

"Did you say it was locked?" asked Griffin.

Cody replied, "Yes," just as Griffin reached down and grabbed a metal bar along the road as he jogged by.

They reached the shed and each circled around in opposite directions.

"There is only the large rollup door and the broken window with bars," said Cody.

Griffin ran his hands along the bars as he looked at the attachment to the building then walked to the door.

Griffin starting slowly, "Even if we open the window, we still need to get the door open, so let's start here. At the padlock."

He inserted the long bar inside the hasp of the lock and tried to pry but the bar slipped out. He muttered to himself, "What's the problem we need to solve? We don't need the lock open. We need the door open."

He moved the bar between the latch and the frame and lifted. As the latch stretched, he adjusted the bar and pushed again. Pop. He smiled at Cody as he rolled the door up.

Lawnmowers, tools, fuel cans, and assorted supplies lined the walls, better than finding treasure.

"Here is a bike pump. I will bring that back for the bikes. Look, batteries!" said Cody.

"They are 12-volt for lawnmowers. How many are there?"

"I see 5, enough to connect in parallel to get enough power for a car, hopefully. Let's test them to see if they have any charge. Do you see a multimeter?

"I don't see a meter but there is a headlight," said Cody.

"Good thinking. Hopefully, the bulb is good."

Griffin grabbed the headlight and a screwdriver from the bench, placed one tab on one battery terminal, and used the screwdriver to connect the second terminal. LIGHT! He moved the setup to the next battery and the next until he got to the fifth battery, which was much dirtier than the others. This time the bulb cast a yellow light.

"I think 4 of these will be enough to start the van but we need to conserve power in the meantime," said Griffin. After thinking a minute, he continued, "Since it's a gasoline engine, it will take less power to start than a diesel with the lower compression ratio, but..." He stopped when he looked at Cody who was not interested in the mechanical details. "It should work. Let's see what else we can use."

They opened cabinets and looked through the items on the bench. Griffin opened a closet door near the entrance and froze.

"Cody!" he called. "There is a generator! It's a small, portable one, but it might be useful. We need to find fuel. We need gasoline for the van and for this thing and propane for the kitchen."

"The kitchen had propane," said Cody. "We turned on the valve and heard a hiss."

"Good to know. Speaking of that, let's run past the warehouse and kitchen and see if we can figure out some breakfast for the group," said Griffin.

The warehouse was nearby and as they turned the corner, they found Maggie.

"Where have you been?" asked Maggie.

"We were checking out the maintenance shed and found a bike pump, batteries, tools, and a generator, but wanted to come see if we could figure out breakfast. Now that I think of it, though, you have the translator so let's find some food. Have you found water?"

"Speaking of water, Brent heard rumbling above the bunkhouse this morning and took Abby up to look for a creek," said Maggie.

"That is great news!" said Cody. "We should grab some of that rice if we think we have water."

"I think I have been running on adrenaline and just realizing how hungry I am," said Maggie.

"Same," said Cody. "We need to get food and water today. Let's grab enough for breakfast and plan to move to the kitchen building today. Actually, let's just take this right to the kitchen and then we can get started while everyone makes their way down from the bunkhouse."

They grabbed a big bag of rice and some assorted cans and Maggie, Cody, and Griffin carried them to the kitchen while Griffin ran up to the bunkhouse with 2 large empty jugs. As he arrived the rest of the group was inside, Shelbi was attending to the bandages. Mia and Cable were mapping the area on foot, Abby and Brent were still gone.

"We found a bunch of good stuff," started Griffin. "Which way did Abby go?"

"We were still laying down when they left, but they said something about a creek up the hill," said Sterling.

Griffin ducked back outside and stood above the bunkhouse and turned his head as he heard the rumbling. After a few head-turns, he loped off with his 2 jugs in the direction of the sound. Soon he was hearing the water more clearly and he noted that he was not hearing the swishing of the water yet. "Must be over a rise," he thought to himself. Standing well over six feet tall, Griffin surveyed the landscape ahead and there was a ridge running parallel to his current path, so he turned up the ridge and pushed his way through the brush. Just as he reached the top and the sound of the water became distinct, he heard a yell coming from the same direction as the water.

His large wingspan fueled by his water polo training spread the branches before him as he leaped over logs through the forest. Hearing another yelp, he adjusted his trajectory and used the plastic jugs in each hand like boxing gloves as he pushed through the willow branches.

"Abby! Brent!" he yelled.

"Here!" he heard Abby yell as he caught sight of her running downstream. "Brent fell in and he is getting pulled downstream! There!" Abby pointed just beyond Griffin. At a full run, Griffin turned slightly, dropped the jugs, and entered the water, no hesitation. The river was deep enough that even Griffin could not reach the bottom in the deeper pools but there were large rocks that created gray obstacles as he was trying to catch up to Brent. Brent was much smaller and not a swimmer, so he was struggling to keep his head above water, let alone trying to get to shore. Griffin pushed through the water and could see that he was gaining on Brent.

"Brent!" he called. "Try to kick toward the shore where the water is slower!"

Brent's head turned a bit, but he did not change direction. Griffin kept pumping and kicking, mid-channel in the river, closing the gap on Brent. A large rock swept Brent to the right, but Griffin was slightly more in the center of the flow and was pushed to the left. The surge pulled Griffin in front of Brent, so he pivoted and in a motion that looked more like a water polo player snatching a ball from an opponent, he caught Brent's collar and pulled him up while kicking hard to the shore. Abby had been following along the shore, fighting her way through willows. Suddenly Griffin rose from the water as he got his feet under him near the shore. Brent was yelling incoherently and not standing, but still supported by Griffin with an arm around his waist. About the time the pair were staggering out of the shallow water, Abby appeared through the bushes and supported the side of Brent.

"My leg!" yelled Brent. "I think it's broken. I can't stand on it."

"Let's sit on this rock," offered Abby.

Griffin was breathing so hard he could not say anything and happy to yield his load to Abby and collapsed on the gravel. Brent winced as he sat down and held his lower leg.

"Looks like," Griffin started before he took another breath. "You found," another breath, "Some water."

Abby chuckled, trying to keep the wavering out of her voice. "Oh, Griff. I'm so glad you arrived when you did and glad you're OK."

"You're glad he's OK? What about me?" blurted Brent.

"You know what I mean," said Abby. "You should have seen him fly into the water."

"I was too busy watching my 15 years flash before me as I was drowning."

Abby had started pulling Brent's right pant leg up and found blood streaming down his wet leg and into his shoe. Griffin was starting to breathe normally and looked around Abby to see Brent's leg. "What's the prognosis, doctor?"

"I don't see anything sticking out, but he is bleeding," answered Abby.

Griffin stood and looked along the river bank. Spotting what he wanted, he walked over and picked up a weathered and flat branch that was a couple feet long. He sat down and pulled off his own shoes and socks. He placed the branch along the outside of Brent's leg from his ankle up to the middle of his thigh. He rolled the end of Brent's pants up over the end of the stick and then tied his socks around Brent's leg near the knee and thigh. He squished his bare feet into his wet shoes.

"Finally, a good use for socks," Griffin said as he stood up. "Let's see if we can get you walking."

Griffin positioned himself on the right side, Abby on the left and they locked arms across each other's shoulders. They struggled through the brush near the shore, but once they got beyond the willows the forest opened a bit and it allowed them to move more freely, albeit slowly. Since they had moved down river during the rescue, they were approaching the park from a different direction and the landmarks were not looking familiar. Eventually, they crested a small ridge.

"I remember this ridge," said Griffin. "This is when I could hear the river more clearly. Oh, dang. I dropped the jugs near the river before I jumped in. I will go back for water after we get back to camp. Let's head this direction and we will eventually hit the park."

As they moved toward where they figured the park would be, they encountered a fence.

"This must be near the public area of the park. We need to move right until we reach our bunkhouse," said Abby.

A few minutes later they encountered a hole in the fence and noticed a road on the other side.

"Let's go through," suggested Griffin. "It should be easier to walk on the road than in this forest."

They maneuvered Brent through the fence and then moved along the road, scanning for buildings and equipment they might find useful.

"What is that?" asked Abby. "It looks like a roller coaster."

"I think it is the back of the one near the bunkhouse because it has the same blue track," said Brent.

"And there is the bunkhouse," pointed Griffin.

They were approaching from the back of the bunkhouse, they couldn't see anyone until they came around the last corner. Shelbi, Sterling, and Mia were all sitting out around the cold remnants of the campfire. Shelbi jumped up, grabbed her crutch and did the best she could to run and greet them.

"What happened to you?" she asked. "Oh, that looks serious. I didn't see the splint at first. And why are you guys all wet?"

"Brent slipped on a rock at the river and Griffin went for a swim," answered Abby.

"Bring him to a bunk. Elevate his leg and get me something like a small pillow, not too thick because we want him to be ready if he goes into shock," instructed Shelbi. "And get him some warm clothes."

They brought Brent inside and laid him down, placed a sweatshirt under his head. Mia brought a blanket she found in a closet and put it over Brent. Shelbi gently lifted his leg and removed the splint and rolled his pant leg up.

"Tell me if you feel sharp pain."

Placing her fingers on either side of his leg, she started at the knee and traced his bones down to his ankle. He winced a few times but nothing severe. Then she untied both shoes and removed the wet socks. She rotated his ankle and then bent his knee.

"It hurts when you press near my knee and when I bend it," said Brent.

Shelbi traced around his kneecap, careful to avoid the bloody abrasions.

"I think you have just clobbered your knee and have contusions, but I don't think any bones are broken. Now we need to get you into dry clothes and need to keep your leg immobile and elevated," diagnosed Shelbi.

"You're amazing Shelbi," noted Abby. "You know all that from first aid training?"

"I have spent some time in hospitals too. I like that splint. Let's see if we find something that will wrap it to his leg better than these two socks. Hand me the First-Aid kit."

"If you are all set here, I am going to get the water," said Griffin as he dashed off around the bunkhouse, his clothes still dripping.

CHAPTER 18 — SETTING UP

"Improvise, Adapt, Overcome" - unofficial slogan, US Marines

By the time that Griffin returned with the water jugs, Brent had changed into dry clothes and had the splint strapped to the side of his leg. Shelbi was attending to him and Sterling and Abby had returned with 2 dollies.

"You've been busy," said Griffin. "I have been thinking about the water. We are not in a grazing area, not even any people; we are collecting water above previous human activity, and the water appears clear. We could boil it to be sure, but I think we could safely drink it. To be honest, I have already downed about a liter plus what I swallowed during my swim with Brent."

"How about you test it for a day, and we will boil it until we know you are ok in 24 hours," suggested Shelbi.

"Listen to you, Doctor Shelbi," said Griffin. "Sounds like a deal. I will run this down to the kitchen to start boiling. Are you ready to start moving bunks?"

Before there was an answer, Griffin dashed to the kitchen with the 2 jugs.

"Let's move bunks," said Abby.

"If we flip the frames over and stack them, we can put them on the dollies and move several at a time," said Brent.

Maggie and Cable had returned from the kitchen during all the mayhem and were at the bunkhouse.

"Good idea," said Maggie. "You rest, and we will start moving."

Flipping the bottom frame and placing it onto 2 dollies, they stacked 4 more frames and mattresses on the frame and started rolling down to the new home by the kitchen. About 30 minutes later, Maggie, Abby, and Cable came running back up the hill with the dollies.

"Brent, we thought about this on the way," said Maggie. "We will move you down the hill on one of these upside-down beds. You too, Sterling. Let's try it."

"Nah. I'm alright," said Brent.

Ignoring him, Cable and Maggie were already flipping the first frame and inserting a mattress between the legs. It even curved up a bit along the edges. Cable crawled on to test it.

"This is great," said Cable. "I might just ride this one down myself for fun. Get on, Brent."

Knowing he was outnumbered, Brent hobbled over and got into the bed frame. Cable hung his legs over the front edge for steering and braking. Maggie and Abby took the back corners and started maneuvering the odd vehicle down the hill.

xiii

With a few more trips the group had moved 9 bunks and everyone down to their new home, DreamLand. It was a staff dining area adjacent to the main kitchen. Griffin had made several trips for water and took Cody with him so there was plenty of water as people arrived.

"I've been drinking the stream water all day, so we should know soon if it is OK," chuckled Griffin. "We still have a couple bottled waters left. Let's eat and figure out our next plans."

"While you were moving the last loads, we found more food cans and other stuff," said Cody. "I also looked at our propane situation and it appears there is one tank that is connected, but no other reserve tanks. It is heavy enough I can't shake it to tell how full it is."

"I'm going to go over to the warehouse to see what type of oil we have over there," said Griffin. "Maggie, would you come with me and bring your translator?"

"Aren't we going to eat first?" asked Maggie.

"Oh, that's right. I'm just excited to see what we have to work with."

"I have started a notebook recording everything we have found so far," said Mia. "I'd like to come with you on the next trip to the warehouse."

They ate the rice and Maggie boiled a can of the mixed vegetables.

"This is the best lunch," exclaimed Cable.

"Isn't it true that everything tastes better when you are hungry?" said Maggie.

"I guess this stuff was more work to carry out of here than it is worth," said Griffin as he fished the last couple kernels of corn from the pot. "Sure glad it worked out that way for us. That bag of rice, alone, will last us a couple weeks."

"I get the feeling that they shut the park down suddenly and then still had some staff here for a while and didn't really clean up after the last employees left. I wonder if it has been closed a year, but the plants have grown quickly," said Cody.

"Maybe they were hoping to open again or come back?" suggested Abby.

"Have you noticed that there aren't very many planes that fly overhead and the ones that do are at full cruising altitude?" asked Mia. "Didn't you say that you were seeing farms and forest before we crashed?"

"Yeah. I don't think any sort of fire or signal would stand out," said Brent.

"Alright," started Griffin. "Maggie and Mia, you two are coming to the warehouse?"

"Since we're pretty much set up, maybe more of us should come and bring the dollies so we can load up and have more on hand at the kitchen in case we get weather," said Cable.

"I will stay with Brent and Sterling," said Shelbi. "and will look around this building for things while you all are gone."

Mia had her notebook and Cable had the dollies. Actually, he was riding one of them like a skateboard and holding the other.

"Please don't fall," advised Mia. "We really can't afford another injury, especially you."

"Good point," said Cable. He hopped off the dolly and carried it. The group entered the warehouse and started opening every cabinet, every box, and every door they could find. Griffin went straight for the barrels to see what was in them.

"Maggie, can you help translate? What's this?" asked Griffin as he pointed at a barrel with the marking, "*гидравлическое.*"

"That's more like Russian with those characters and I did not bring a Russian translator," answered Maggie.

"There's a few of them so I will open one and smell it."

"Why does that not surprise me?" asked Mia as she came around the corner with her notebook.

Griffin spun the large cap and slowly bent his head near the opening while sniffing.

"Almost no smell, so it is not very volatile," said Griffin.

"Meaning?" asked Mia.

"It is probably just hydraulic oil for the coasters, not fuel. Fuel will smell stronger, but..." Griffin trailed off. "I wonder what our little van can burn. Generator. We need to find gasoline for the generator."

"Slow down. One thing at a time. How many barrels with this marking?" asked Mia who was writing in her notebook.

"Looks like 4," said Griffin. "But there are 2 more of a different color behind those against the wall."

"*Petrolej*!" shouted Griffin. "Maggie, what's *petrolej*? I like the sound of it and the characters don't look Russian. P-E-T-R-O-L-E-J"

"Kerosene," said Maggie.

"Yee-hah, that will work," said Griffin. "In the van and generator, anyway."

"So, that's 2 barrels of kerosene and 4 barrels of mystery Russian oil?" asked Mia as she wrote.

"Let's leave all the non-food items here and focus on only taking food back to base camp," said Griffin. "Now that we might have fuel, I want to get back to the van with those batteries to see if we can start it."

After finding a few wood crates, they loaded cans, bags, and boxes of food items and pushed them on the dollies back to base camp.

Cody was looking at the pot they were using to boil water.

"Do you remember the stove that Mr. Alpin showed us on the camping trip?" asked Cody.

"Ya, the Jetboil that had the heat exchanger fins on the..." Cable trailed off. "I see where you are going. We have limited fuel so if we increase the surface area of our pot, we can use less fuel to boil the same water. At a minimum, we should use the thin metal pot and shield the flame. I will work on it." Cable ran off.

"I am going to take the batteries to the van to see if I can get the gauges lit up," said Griffin. "Abby, would you come with?"

"Sure," said Abby and they got up to leave just has Cable came back in carrying a piece of ducting sheet metal.

"Cody, where's the pot? I want to see if this will focus the heat," said Cable.

"I also found a better pot," said Cody. It has an aluminum bottom, a little bit bigger in diameter. Here."

Cable turned the pot over, carried it and the sheet metal to the stove.

"Efficiency is all about moving the most energy from the fuel to the water," muttered Cable to himself as if instructing his own class or recalling one from school. "The energy required is determined by the amount and temperature of the water to be boiled." Raising his voice for others to hear, "We should get some tanks to put the cold stream water into so that the water warms up a bit in the sun to decrease our fuel usage," Then, dropping back to his internal voice, "Energy transmitted to the pot will be determined by the surface area of the pot, temperature difference, and," he paused, "the color of the pot. Shiny is bad. Black is good. OK," he seemed to confirm to himself. "I am going to go look for sheet metal shears in the workshop."

Griffin and Abby were carrying the last 2 batteries and had pockets stuffed with wires and a couple of tools when Cable came into the shop.

"Have you seen any sheet metal shears?" asked Cable.

"Ya, there's stuff like that in that toolbox," said Abby as she was headed out with her hands full.

"I wonder what Cable is working on," said Abby to Griffin as they carried their load to the van.

"Probably his pot heat exchanger," said Griffin. "I have been thinking about this battery issue. We need to connect these in parallel, right? Series would increase the voltage and we need the same 12 volts but with more current."

"Yep. I always have to think about that too."

"Parallel means we stack the batteries and connect all the terminals on the right and all the ones on the left. We could just use 2 strips of metal with 4 holes each. Otherwise, we need big wire to take the current draw. For now, we just need one battery to turn on the gauges."

They set the 2 batteries on the ground next to the van with the first 2. Griffin removed the engine cover and peered inside and grabbed the battery cable.

"These are a standard car terminal post clamp and the batteries have the metal tabs with small screws. Maybe you can just hold these on while I turn on the ignition switch to see the gauges."

"Sure, Griff."

"I need to look at the ignition wires first to see if I can tell which one is which."

Griffin opened the door and was twisting his long body upside down to look under the dash. He pulled a few wires in the small bundle. He flipped over on his back and slid until his head was looking up behind the metal dash panel.

"Ah," he said. "The blue wire appears to go to the center and the yellow, orange, and red come from the switch, but they are the same size, so I don't know which one is for accessories and which is ignition. But, they are in order so maybe we have accessories, fuel pump, then ignition. Go ahead and hold the battery cables to the terminals and I will just spark them to find which one we want."

"Ready," called Abby.

"Here goes the blue to yellow," replied Griffin. "Small spark and no noise. Let me connect these."

He grabbed a wire from his pocket and a pair of pliers. He cut a few centimeters off and stripped a bit of insulation off each end.

Laying on his back, he slid under the dash and twisted the wires around the blue and yellow terminals while a small spark danced between his fingers. He quickly sat up in the seat and looked at the gauges.

"We have gauges! Fuel is about half full! Temperature is cold, voltage is 11ish, and oil gauge not reading, as expected. I can't wait. Let's get those batteries connected. OK, disconnect the battery for now."

"This is a gas engine, which means I want to run a fuel pump for a second and then the starter. I need a way to connect them in order and not all at the same time. Let's go get some metal to join the batteries."

"I have been looking at the battery tray and these batteries and I think we can fit 3 batteries on the tray but the fourth one won't fit unless we strap it over there," Abby said as she pointed to an open area next to the battery tray.

"We could try using just 3 batteries," said Griffin. "I was thinking about it and it only has 4 cylinders so with the lower compression of the gas engine will be easier with—"

"Only 4 cylinders," Abby finished his sentence. "Good thinking. Let's go get the power rails."

Just as Griffin and Abby were coming back to the shed Cable was exiting with his sheet metal masterpiece. "I am going to try out my new heat chimney," said Cable.

"Did you find any sheet metal strips and shears?" asked Griffin.

"The shears are in the toolbox. I just put them back after making a modification and there is lots of scrap metal around the back. That is where I found the ducting."

Abby darted around the shed to the back and Griffin went inside for the tools. After finding the shears he was hearing some crashing and banging around back and found Abby knee deep in metal remnants. She was holding a copper strap and smiling.

"I think this will be heavy enough for the current and yet thin enough for us to cut," she said.

Without another word, they were jogging back to the van, both running mental lists and designs through their heads.

As they arrived at the van, they simultaneously started,

"Let-"

"How about-"

"Go ahead," said Griffin.

"Let's just cut small notches for the bolts and slip the strap over the studs and tighten the nuts," said Abby.

"Great idea," he said. "I will run back for a wrench to tighten the nuts. We still need a way to attach the terminal post clamps to the sheet metal. Hey, will the clamp slit fit over the sheet metal? Maybe if we spread it with a screwdriver. I will be right back."

Abby put the batteries into the compartment behind the driver's seat and then held the strap up to the terminals for sizing. She cut one strap to length and then cut notches for each stud. After making 2 of them and seeing how the battery cables would fit Griffin appeared through the passenger door with a wrench in hand.

"Do you have the flat screwdriver?" asked Abby. "I need to spread the clamp a bit to fit over the strap."

"Yep, here," replied Griffin as he inserted the tip into the clamp and twisted as Abby pushed it onto the new power rails. "We should probably put something over these rails in case anything drops behind the seat and shorts across."

Abby tightened the nuts on the 6 studs and looked at Griffin. "Can we try to start it?"

"I have been thinking that we just need to extend the blue, yellow, orange, and red wires so that we can connect them while sitting in the seat," said Griffin.

"I will make 4 wires, about a foot long," said Abby.

Griffin twisted his body and looked up behind the dash as Abby handed him wires. He paused and then said, "What's the problem we are trying to solve? We don't actually need an ignition switch. We just need to connect these wires." He pulled then spun the nut off the back of the ignition switch and it landed on his chest. He pushed the 4 wires out through the hole.

Sitting where the seat would be, Griffin pressed the clutch pedal then first touched the blue to yellow wire and the dash lit up. Next, he added the orange wire and heard and chugging sound and removed the orange wire.

"That would have been too easy to have them in color order," he said.

Leaving the yellow wire in place, he added the red wire and a single light appeared on the dash. "Fuel pump and accessories. Now pray," he said.

Adding the orange wire, there was suddenly a loud chugging, knocking, and rattling since they were essentially sitting inside the engine compartment with the doghouse removed. It sputtered a few times. Suddenly, the engine rumbled to a steady clickety hum of a small engine. Griffin and Abby looked at each other.

"Get in," said Griffin as Abby ran to the passenger side and hopped in. "Stick shift! I should have thought about this more before starting it." He looked at the top of the shifter to see the pattern. "Top left," he said as he jiggled it into position. He touched the accelerator and the rattle sped up. He eased the clutch out and increased the throttle until the van lurched out of its weed encrusted parking spot.

The van clamored its way up the lane, huffing and puffing black smoke.

"Let's drive around DreamLand building and then park it near the shed so it is close to the tools and nearer to our camp," suggested Abby.

"OK, here we go."

As the van came around the corner near the mess hall, everyone came outside to see what was making the great racket. Even Brent stood up to see as the van drove by the door and circled the building.

"Wooohoooo," yelled Cable.

Cable chased the van until it came to rest in front of the shed and gave a high five to Abby and Griffin. They walked back to DreamLand chatting excitedly about the details of installing the batteries and starting it up. Everyone was still standing outside in midday sun as everything seemed a bit brighter and cheerier than before.

CHAPTER 19 — WATER

Water is the driving force of all nature. - Leonardo da Vinci

"I can't believe you got that van to run," said Sterling. "I had accepted that we were going to die here, but now I have hope."

"You have to hold onto hope," said Maggie. "Let's run through our plan. We haven't seen any search planes, or any low-flying planes, so we figure that they don't know where we are. We have a van that runs, thanks to Griff and Abby. We appear to be on the shore of a lake that has no exit except across the lake, so we need a way across, and we need to find a way to float us plus the van that weighs how much?"

"I figure about 4000 pounds or 1800 kilos. We are 9 times 130 pounds or another 1200 pounds or 540 kilos, so we are 2300 kilos for us and the van. At 1 gram per 1 cubic centimeter the mass equals 2.3 cubic meters of water. A 55-gallon drum is about 200 liters or .2 cubic meters, so we need about 12 55-gallon drums to float us and the van across the lake."

"Been thinking about this much, Griff?" asked Brent.

"How big do you think those log ride boats are?" asked Cable.

"Hmm, without measuring I would guess about 3 barrels," said Brent.

"Don't forget that we can't submerge them completely, so we only get to use about half the displaced volume," said Cable.

"And we need to remember the weight of the logs," reminded Maggie.

"Ugh," said Griffin. "I was getting excited about only needing 4 logs and we are more like 8. And, we still need a way to propel 2300 kg through the water."

"What motors have we found so far?" asked Mia. "I have written down the van and 2 bicycles, but nothing else."

"There was a motorcycle somewhere, right?" asked Cable.

"Yes, near the warehouse, but it was missing the front wheel, but we don't need wheels. We need a propeller," said Griffin, his voice trailed off to think about propellers, driveshafts, and chain drives from the solar boat project they worked on the year before.

"While Brent and Griff were going for a swim, Mia and I explored as many roads as we could find and she made a map in her notebook," said Cable. "Basically, we are in one valley between two ridges. We did not find any roads that go over either ridge. The river is to the east of the ridge."

Mia continued, "One thing I have been thinking about is they needed water when they ran this park and I bet they either ran a pipe upstream or tapped into a spring and fed a tank. We did not find the tank yet, but it must be higher than the park and it is hard to see up into the forest. I wonder if we can find it and get water restored, at least to the kitchen."

"Good thinking," said Maggie. Any guesses about where the tank might be?"

"The only river we know about is the one Brent and Abby found to the east. Could you see anything to the west?" asked Griffin.

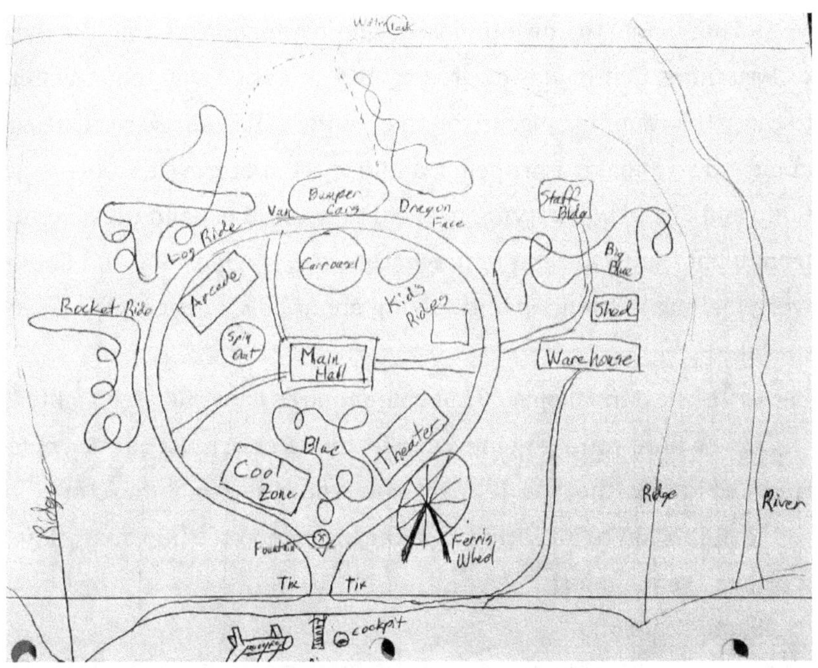

"We went down to the shore near the plane and couldn't see past where the west ridge hits the shore," said Cable. "From that, we could surmise the tank would be fed out of the east river up high enough that it would feed a tank above the staff quarters or the Dragon Face coaster."

"I don't think the staff quarters ridge area is high enough, so I think Dragon Face is a better shot. I can go up there to look sometime," said Griffin. "I have been using a trail that goes roughly east, above the warehouse to get over a lower part of the ridge to the river for water."

No one had noticed that Shelbi had gone inside, but she emerged and announced, "Lunch is ready. We will be serving mixed veggie rice today."

"Mixed veggie rice! My favorite," joked Cable.

During lunch, the group plotted and planned. Now that the van was running, Griffin was excited to find an easier way to get water to camp than running jugs to the river. Abby and Brent were chatting about how to make a propeller and use the motorcycle to drive it. Cody and Shelbi were trying to see if they could expand their menu from what they had seen in the warehouse. Maggie, Mia, and Cable were looking at the map and talking about how to get log boats to the lake.

"Griff," started Maggie. "That ride requires a lot of water, right?"

"I see where you are going," said Griffin. "There must be a big pipe from the tank to the ride. It might point me in the right direction."

"Griff, I want to go with you to the log ride to see how many logs we have," said Cable.

"Same," said Mia.

"I will go with Abby to see if we can find a propeller," said Maggie.

Griffin held his hand out facing the sun and spread his fingers and counted, "We have another 4 hours of daylight so let's get going. And those clouds are looking dark."

"I will grab my notebook," said Mia as she and Cable stood to join him.

"Let's start at the log ride and work our way up the hill if we find a pipe," said Griffin.

The log ride was a short walk due east of DreamLand. Everyone was quiet as they walked, thinking about pipes, gravity, and hoping that they could find the puzzle pieces of this next challenge.

"So, it looks like the ride has a staging area down by the lines but there is sort of a boathouse behind. Let's climb up to get a bird's eye view," said Griffin. "We can get on the roof over here."

Griffin loped over to the vine-covered trellis and reached up and pulled himself onto the roof of the waiting area shelter. "Do you want to come up?"

"No, let us know what you see," said Mia. "We will work our way along the loading area."

"Here are 2 logs in the main channel," yelled Cable.

xiv

"I can see the 6 in the boathouse area from up here," said Griffin. "Wait, I think I see a couple more in the channel behind the boat shed. It is hard to get there from where you are so let me look."

Griffin leaped from roof to roof and worked his way to the top of the boat shed.

"There are 2 more back here but one is sunken. That means we have 10. I will jump down over here. Oh, I see a pipe heading through the brush up the hill and to the east. That's a good sign."

By the time that Mia and Cable made their way through the brush to the boatshed area, Griffin was jumping down next to the 8 log boats.

"I bet we could get 1 of these in the van at a time to get them down to the water," said Griffin. They measure about 1 meter in diameter and only the top 20 centimeters or so is cut off, so we have good buoyancy. These are almost 2.5 meters long, but the water volume is about 2 meters."

Mia was writing everything down. "That is just about 1.5 cubic meters per boat without the cutout," said Mia. "If we deduct one third for the top, we get about 1 cubic meter per boat. That is more than we were thinking. Let me make sure. .5 times .5 is .25. Pi times 2 is about 6 so .25 times 6 is 1.5. That means we only need about 3 boats."

"We should use 4 for stability. Do you think we can keep a van stable on top of 4 logs?" asked Griffin. "The van is about 4.4 meters long so it would just be barely shorter than 2 logs. I would feel better if we had more stability. Let's go over the geometry and loads back at camp. I saw the pipe heading that direction. If we go through the boatshed, we can avoid the fence."

"Let's go," said Cable.

Mia just folded her notebook and ran to keep up. The hill climbed steeply behind the ride and was covered in brush and trees. Griffin's long legs vaulted over many obstacles that Cable and Mia had to jump and weave through, so Griffin remained several paces ahead. That worked well for everyone because he was able to see forward and direct the other two. They moved slowly up the hill following glimpses of the white pipe.

"Look, a tee-fitting that points down to the main park," said Griffin. There are shut-off ball valves, too, and everything is closed. Let's keep heading up the hill along the main line."

Sweat dripped from Cable's nose. Leaves and dirt stuck to Mia's face. They looked at each other, dipped their heads down, and followed Griffin.

"There!" shouted Griffin as he pointed up the hill at a white shadow that was appearing through the trees. "Let's circle around to the right and come up the ridge. It looks a little clearer and less steep."

A few minutes later and the three of them had reached the ridge and worked their way up to the tank. They sat down with their backs to the cool metal tank. Cable picked up a small rock and tapped the tank.

"Sounds full, not hollow," said Griffin.

Griffin rolled over and crawled around the corner.

"There is a black poly pipe that feeds this tank, an overflow pipe, a drain valve, and an outlet valve. Can you help me open the drain?" asked Griffin.

Cable hopped up and the two walked to the back of the tank. A few minutes later and a stream of cool water shot out from behind the tank.

"Woohoo, we have water!" shouted Cable. "Now, let's see if we can get it down to DreamLand. Ugh, down. Is there anything else we should do while we are up here?"

"I noticed an overflow pipe that heads back down toward the creek," said Griffin. "It looks like this has been feeding and flowing through the whole time, so the water should be fresh."

They started heading back down the hill, retracing their steps.

"It's a lot easier going down than up," said Cable as he led the group downhill.

Suddenly Cable disappeared under the large leaves and they heard bumps and moans coming through the brush.

"Cable! Are you ok?" called Griffin.

"Ya, sort of," they heard Cable moan below them.

They made their way down the muddy hillside and found Cable upside down in the brush.

"Whatcha doin', resting?" joked Griffin. "Does anything hurt like it is broken?"

"Na, gimme a hand."

Mia and Griffin got Cable standing back up, brushed him off, and checked his head for injuries.

"I recommend a shower," said Mia.

Cable chuckled. "Let's go."

"The tee-fitting is just ahead," said Griffin. I have been thinking that maybe we open the valve to the park and listen for the flow."

Griffin got to the valve first and rotated the ball valve with minor effort. He put his ear to the pipe then adjusted his head and cupped his hands around his ear.

"I heard a lot of flow at first, but I don't hear anything except maybe a trickle," said Griffin.

"There is more of a trail heading down along the main pipe vs the way we came from the log ride," said Mia. "I didn't notice it on the way up, but do you see the path that direction?"

"Yep, let's see if we have water now," said Cable.

They worked their way down the overgrown path and ended up under a tall roller coaster track on the hill.

"Is this Dragon Face?" asked Mia. "If it is, then we are at the top of the park and the bumper cars will be down to the right and DreamLand is straight below."

"Here is the fence," said Cable. "Let's follow the pipe but head to the right and come up between here and the bumper cars."

The pipe ran through the fence and under the roller coaster, but they followed the perimeter around until it reached a point that was closer to the road and there was a service gate. It was locked but easier to climb than the fence.

"Since we are so close let's just head back to the kitchen to see if we have water," said Mia.

"Good idea," said Griffin.

They rounded the carousel and entered the kitchen through the back service entrance.

"Look," said Cable. "It's dripping. The faucet's dripping."

He reached for the lever and pulled. Water splashed and spurted, red-brown water and foamy air blasted into the sink. After a few minutes, the water ran clear.

"Do you realize what it means if air was still trapped in the pipe?" asked Griffin.

"That it did not come out somewhere else," answered Mia.

"There should not be any leaks and nothing else is open in the system," said Cable.

"Oh my gosh! Is that water ok to drink?" asked Shelbi as she hobbled into the kitchen.

"We should let it run a while, but the tank system looks good," said Griffin.

Clear water continued to pour into the sink. Cody came into the kitchen.

"Water!" exclaimed Cody.

"Are Maggie and Abby still gone?" asked Cable.

"Ya, looking for a prop," said Cody.

"I thought of an idea. Are the bikes still out front?" asked Cable as he walked out.

"Yep, and we filled the tires," said Cody.

Cable hopped on a bike and headed down the hill. His first stop was the Ferris wheel. He moved to the equipment room at the base of the tower. Luckily the door was unlocked so he opened it, looking in front and behind the main drive motor for the fan. "About 24 inches in diameter, pretty big," he mumbled to himself.

He mounted the bike and headed past the Cool Zone and turned right to the equipment room for the small blue coaster. This equipment room was more of a cage with a padlock. He circled around to the back. "Ah, about 12 inch and sturdy blades," he murmured. He grabbed the shovel he found leaning against the back of the Cool Zone and placed the round tip between the frame and the door of the cage. The door bent slightly. Seeing the weakness, he adjusted the shovel position near the bottom of the door and pushed and the door moved enough that he was able to get the head of the shovel in the gap. Grabbing the door, bending his knees and placing his feet against the frame he extended his legs and pressed the door enough to get his body through the opening. He moved back to the end of the cage with the fan and studied the connections. "Phillips driver for the guard and sockets to remove the fan hub," he noted. He hopped on the bike and continued his circle looking for Maggie and Abby and encountered them on the road back to DreamLand.

"Did you find any propellers?" asked Cable.

"Not really," answered Maggie.

"We went to the shore but did not find any boats and then we were at the log ride looking for any pumps, but they all seemed more like water jets," said Abby.

"I got to thinking. Do you remember that class where we talked about flow dynamics?" asked Cable. "We talked about kinematic viscosity and the way that air is a fluid and many of the equations apply for fluid flow. I remember that the viscosity factor was something like a factor of 10 to 20 times higher for water and that if we rotate an air fan at one 15th the speed in water we should get good flow. I found a fan about the size of the prop we use for the solar-powered boat but with 6 blades. I am wondering if we removed 3 and turned it slower, we might have a prop."

"I do remember that and 15 sounds familiar. Would that mean it would be about one 8th the speed if we remove half the blades?" asked Maggie.

"I think we need to test it," said Abby. How about we test it before removing the blades and then decide? I have seen 6 blade props when I go boating with my dad."

"How about we grab one of the props from the plane?" proposed Griffin with a smile. "I think the one on the left is fine. We could use the fuel and the engine and really fly across the water."

"Except the engine probably weighs as much as the van and we don't have a crane, or control system, or welder, but other than that it's perfect," said Cable.

Having water in the kitchen was a huge boost to everyone and good timing, all the water bottles from the plane had been used. The empty bottles had all been saved by Mia, not really knowing if they might come in handy or just following habits of recycling.

As the group was finishing dinner, the conversation continued on point.

"Mia, what have you recorded for the motors we found?" asked Griffin.

"The van – gasoline, 4-cylinder Motorcycle – no front wheel, unknown condition. Generator – gas, unknown condition. Lawnmowers. I think that is it," answered Mia.

"What about fuel?" asked Brent.

"2 barrels of kerosene and 4 barrels of unknown oil, probably hydraulic," answered Mia.

"Griff, can we run a gasoline engine on kerosene?" asked Brent.

"Now that you mention it, I researched that last summer and was surprised that it worked pretty well, but it needs a bit of tuning," answered Griffin. "We can run the motorcycle on the kerosene, too. We could probably retrieve some Jet A fuel from the plane if we wanted to, but I think we have enough kerosene."

"Then we have a way to run the propeller for thrust on a raft," finished Maggie.

"Tomorrow I will work on seeing if the motorcycle will run," said Griffin.

"Brent, how are you healing up?" asked Maggie.

"My knee hurts, but Shelbi was right. I don't think there are any broken bones. I won't be able to do any heavy lifting, or even walking for now, but I want to help with the engineering. I have some ideas about how we should make the motor and propeller system."

"And how are you doing Sterling?" asked Abby.

"I, I'm OK. I am really banged up and still can't really stand for long, but you kids have been amazing. Thank you. I am still in shock about Rick, the man I was with on the plane. He is married and no one knows he was on this trip..."

The room was quiet as everyone was trying to fill in the blanks and not say the wrong thing.

"I am so sorry for your loss," said Maggie. Of course, Maggie knew what to say.

"Now that we are more settled maybe we can go back to the plane tomorrow to get your big bag out, or at least the stuff," said Cable.

"That would be great. I have only had a few things from my carry-on bag. As I think about it, I don't need everything, just the main clothes section. I have been watching all of you strip away every problem you encounter and focus on real problems. You don't get distracted by secondary, unimportant things. Shelbi has been taking care of me like one of your own." Sterling paused. "The people in my world are not like you. I see that now. Let me know how I can help."

"Sterling, we are glad to have you with us," said Cable. "I will see what we can bring back for you. I will also take a Phillips driver and see if we can find a socket set to get the fan off that blower."

"I will go with you," said Abby. "I can bring my duffel with us to use to move things."

"So, for tomorrow it sounds like Griff and Brent will work on the motorcycle," said Maggie. "Cable and Abby will go to the plane. Look for any other useful stuff while you are there."

"Already thinking about it," said Abby.

CHAPTER 20 – RAFTS AND MOTORS

Ideas are like rabbits. You get a couple and learn how to handle them, and pretty soon you have a dozen. - John Steinbeck

Thunder rumbled in the early morning light.

"Griff, is there anything we need to do before it rains?" asked Abby, hiding her concern.

Griffin whispered, "The van and the shed door are closed. I want to work on the motorcycle today and the tools are in the shed, and Brent wants to help but he can't get around much. Without a wheel, it is tough to move the motorcycle and it is already near the shed so maybe he can work on something here and I can get Cody or Maggie to come with me."

"Sounds like we should get going, I don't want to be digging around the plane in the rain."

As Abby and Griffin started moving around and eating, the rest of the group awoke. A rumble of thunder launched Maggie, Cable, and Cody out of bed.

"Looks like we might get rain, so we want to get an early start," said Abby. "Cable, if you are coming with me to the plane, maybe Cody or Maggie can join Griff at the shed with the bike."

"If we are getting rain, maybe I will go straight to get the fan propeller and Cody can help you at the plane," said Cable.

"I can come with you, Griff," said Maggie.

"Brent, can you and Mia work here to figure out how to join at least four of the logs so we can support the van and all 9 of us?" asked Abby. "The tough part is that we have not found a welder, nor do we have a powerful generator, so we need to join the parts in some other way."

"Sure," said Brent. "Not like I can run around in the rain pushing a motorcycle anyway."

"I will come with you to the shed to get some tools and then head to the small blue coaster," said Cable. "Let's get going."

Everyone rolled out to their chosen tasks. Shelbi checked on Sterling's bandages and Brent's knee.

"What if we used the bed frames to link all the logs?" asked Shelbi. "They are already welded, sturdy as army beds, and about the right length to bridge from one log to another."

"That might just work. The logs are," Mia paused as she was looking at her notes. "1 meter in diameter and the beds are just over 2 meters long. There is a steel pipe rail along either side of the opening so we could tie the end of the bed frame to the rail and have the logs separated a bit for stability."

"I like this," said Brent, with a lopsided smile, "and it wasn't even my idea. Have you seen any materials that would make a good deck for the van?"

"Do we need a deck?" asked Shelbi. "What's the problem we need to solve? We just need a place to support 4 wheels and 9 people. Seems like we just need 2 ramps. Do you think we should ride in the van? If the raft fails halfway across the lake, I am not sure we want to be in a metal coffin."

"Fair point," said Brent. "If the ramps were wide enough, we could stand along the outside of the van on either side, so we just need 2 ramps that are about half a meter wide. Maybe use some doors or tables or benches."

"The wood dining tables in the pavilion are at least 3 meters long and a meter wide so maybe we can take them apart and split them," said Shelbi.

"I will go measure them," said Mia.

"I think you just designed our raft," said Brent. "We could use rope or wire to lash the frames at both sets of rails to prevent the logs from rolling and then put some spacer that is about half a meter wide between the logs. How about we use each set with 2 logs and the frames on top, but how should we join 2 full sets? Will the table planks be enough? I am picturing that the lake will have waves and roll the raft. We either need to be stiff enough to act as one plank or flexible enough to let the 4 corners ride up and down and not fall apart."

"Let's do it like the independent suspension of that Baja Racer robot we worked on last year," said Shelbi. "The van is probably pretty rigid, so the 4 wheels will be mostly like a plane. Maybe we just need to lash each wheel to the frames. Or better, maybe we lash each wheel all the way to the logs through the frames."

"The planks are just over 3 meters long, about 10 feet like that Baltic birch plywood we used in class," said Mia as she returned from the dining area. "The planks are 5-6 cm thick and are bolted with hex bolts so we should be able to use the socket set that Cable is getting to take them apart and even use the holes for our ropes. I will work on some sketches."

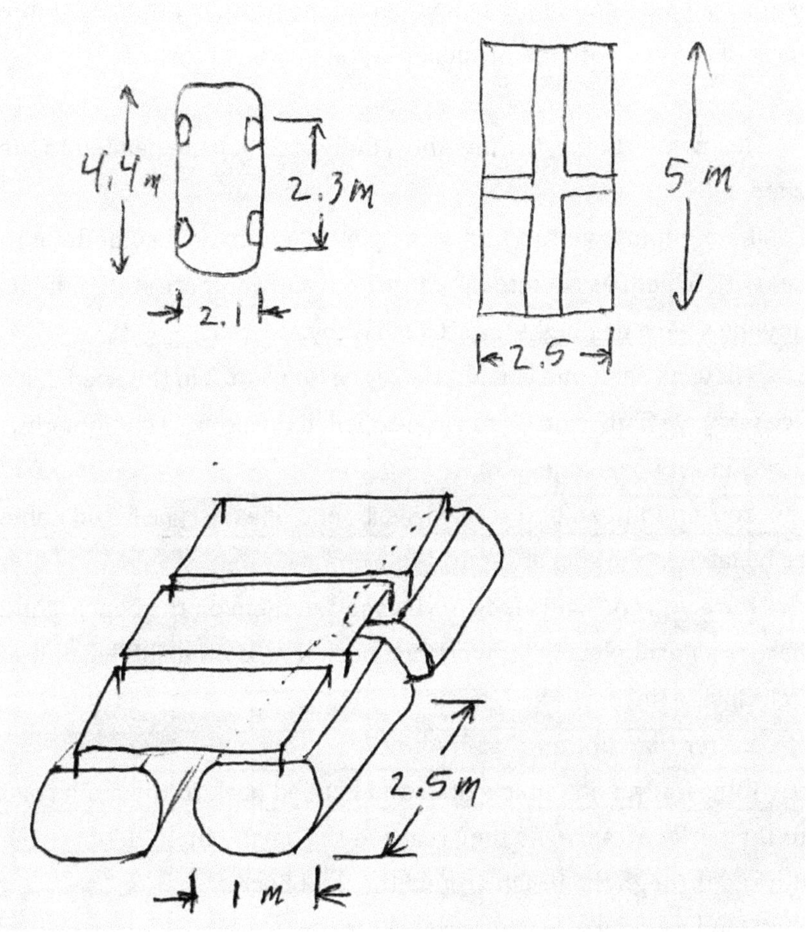

"Maybe, instead of 2 bedframes per set we put one frame under the front axle, one that connects the front logs to the back logs, and a third frame under the rear axle," suggested Brent.

"Perfect," said Shelbi. "It's weird how you are suggesting ideas instead of telling everyone that your way is the only way, I like it."

"We need a way to support the motorcycle," said Mia, ignoring the comments about Brent. "Most are chain driven and the rotation is perpendicular to the bike so it would need to be attached to the back of the van with the propeller in the middle of the raft."

Meanwhile, Cable, Griffin, Abby, Cody, and Maggie headed to the shed.

"I am hoping we can find some gloves and maybe something to cut with to help us get into the cargo hold and get more stuff out. Has anyone seen a flashlight too?" asked Abby.

"I haven't seen one yet, but there is a lot of stuff in the shed. Let's see what we find," said Griffin as he opened the door. "That looks like a socket set box, Cable."

"Yep, and I need two screwdrivers, one of each type," said Cable as he latched the socket set lid.

"Here you go," said Maggie who spotted them on the bench. "And here is a flashlight. Will it work?" It hesitated, then dribbled a bit of light inside the dark shed.

"Better than nothing," said Abby.

Abby, Cody, and Cable exited and headed back to the main road to the park entrance. As they reached the small blue coaster, Cable ducked through the brush around the Cool Zone.

"Good luck and see you soon," said Cable.

After trying a couple of sockets, he found the one that fit the nut on the fan shaft. "I wonder if this is a reverse thread," muttered Cable as he set the torque direction on the wrench and pulled in the counterclockwise direction. Nothing budged except the motor turned a bit, giving a false hope that the nut had loosened. "I need an impact," he said to himself as he moved back out of the cage and spied a rock. After lining up the wrench again, he struck the end of the wrench and it didn't move. He switched the torque direction and placed the wrench on the nut. He moved his fingers out of the way and struck the end of the handle and it seemed to move. With another strike, he was sure that it moved so he dropped the rock and pulled with all his might and the nut rotated off. "Hmm, reverse thread," he confirmed to himself. The fan did not pull off, so he placed each screwdriver on either side of the hub and pried with both simultaneously. He adjusted the drivers and pried again. The fan popped loose. "I wonder what we will use as a shaft. This one is part of the motor." He gathered the tools and fan and maneuvered out of the cage to head back to the shed with his catch of the day. Leaving the fan and socket set at the edge of the road, he admired the dark clouds that were curling over the mountain and picked up his pace to a jog toward the plane.

At first, Cable could not see or hear anything as he approached the plane.

"Abby, Cody!" called Cable.

"We are inside," replied Cody. "Can you give us a hand to pull out what we have? The duffle is sitting out there with the missing small pack."

Cody started passing rolled-up clothes through the mess of wires and debris to Cable, who stuffed everything into the duffle.

"Do you think it is worth trying to get our Pelican cases out with our project? It's not like adaptive control and vibration suppression will help, but it feels strange to just leave it."

"I don't think the cases will fit but let's try," said Abby. "They are half the size of Sterling's black bag. That lady can pack."

After some maneuvering and cutting, the case was pushed all the way to Cable, followed by the second one.

"Is there anything else that would be useful?" asked Cable.

"It's pretty empty, except for the black bags and debris," replied Abby. "Let's go look in the forward section."

Everyone had been avoiding the forward section, but it could hold valuable or useful materials.

"Why do you think no one has come looking for us?" asked Cody.

"I have been thinking about that," said Cable. "The plane had electrical issues before takeoff and then when I woke up, we were flying really low over remote forest areas. I wonder if they lost electrical systems and transponders and were flying too low through the mountains to have good radar signature."

"You really have been thinking about it," said Abby. "I have been thinking the same thing. It is a smaller plane and probably does not have the radar signature or all the tracking systems that the 777 has. It's not like they can lose an entire Malaysian 777, right? Oh, wait, that did happen."

They stopped talking as they arrived at the forward mass of twisted metal and final resting place of at least three people. Birds were circling the metal structure, a few were perched on the top shards of aluminum.

"When Maggie and I came down here the first time, we did not try to get into the cockpit area," said Cody. "I still would rather not."

"I will try to climb up to see if there is anything worth retrieving," said Cable as he started to reach up and lift himself up through a mass of swinging debris. As he got up to the first level of the post-apocalyptic climbing structure and reached for the next bar, a swarm of birds squawked their way out of the ruins and startled Cable.

"I don't think there is anything that we want here," said Cable. "I think that the only thing that anyone wants is for the birds."

Cody, Abby, and Cable carried the 2 Pelican cases, a duffle full of Sterling's clothes, a small backpack, and a couple cell phone chargers up the beach, through the entrance where Cable retrieved the fan and tools. Cable turned to take the fan to the shed and the others returned to the DreamLand just as raindrops started dotting the old pavement.

As Cable entered the shed, he found Griffin and Maggie sitting on the ground next to the motorcycle that they had propped up and clamped between two sawhorses. They were holding sprockets in midair as if they were operating on an invisible machine.

"Here is the fan that seems like the best fit so far," said Cable.

"Great," said Maggie. "We are just puzzling about how to hold the propeller shaft from the two fork supports and allow a shaft to extend to the water."

Griffin continued, "The problem is that the motorcycle wheels are designed to have the axle bolt be on the non-rotating side that is attached to the fork and all the rotating section is on the outer race and trapped between the forks. We need an axle rotating outside the forks."

"Do we even know if the bike runs?" asked Cable.

"Sort of," said Griffin. "We put kerosene in it and cranked it over and it sort of ran. It will need some tuning."

"Let's back out and see what we need and what we have," said Cable. "We need a propeller to spin under water. We have a motorcycle that has a motor output and a chain. How do we transmit rotation that is above water to a propeller that is under water? Let's think outside the bike frame for a minute. We don't need to spin a propeller. We just need to have propulsion. What are other ways to get propulsion in water?"

"Paddlewheel," said Maggie.

"Pump and jet," said Griffin.

Rain thundered on the tin roof of the shed, the only sound as the three engineers sat and pondered how to move something through water.

"So, we have 3 different systems," said Cable. "I can't think of any others, so we have the traditional propeller that mounts with the axle in the direction of travel. The paddlewheel that runs transverse and the jet needs some specialized hardware to produce pressure and thrust inside a pump and we direct that flow out the rear. We might find something we can use at the log ride, but I suspect they used a centralized pump and directed the flow via hoses. It is easy enough to check out. Maybe we should work on all 3 designs before we start taking apart the motorcycle."

"Have you found any useful parts in here that would help us with shafts, sprockets, pumps, or anything else?" asked Cable.

"There are some of those parts on the rack along the back wall," said Maggie as she gestured behind Cable.

Cable stood and started picking up each part, examining it and categorizing each one for its potential design application.

"Griff, you are a swimmer," started Cable. "How long would it take you to swim across the lake?"

"I, I thought about that, but then we don't know what's on the other side. I have looked at night for any lights and I have seen nothing, so even if I did swim across, I may not find anything and still not have food, shelter or transportation."

The rain suddenly tapered off and it was quiet except for a few birds that announced the break in the storm.

"Let's run back and have some lunch," suggested Maggie.

The sun peeked through the clouds and each leaf and blade of grass was trimmed in diamonds.

"As creepy as this place is, it really can be beautiful at the same time," said Maggie. "Not that I will miss it or anything when we go back home." She paused in thought. "I miss home. I miss not having to survive each day. But, I cannot think of better people to be surviving with."

"Same," said Cable.

They entered DreamLand to find bedframes reorganized into 6 frames and some blankets draped over them crosswise and carboys underneath. Cable set down the socket set and screwdrivers.

"What?" started Griffin. "Are you building a fort?"

"No, no. This is our raft frame assembly," blurted Brent excitedly. "And Shelbi designed it."

All eyes turned to Shelbi, who looked at the ground then said, "There would be 4 logs arranged 2 across and 2 in-line with these carboys between. The bed legs would rest just inside the logs and get attached to the pipe rails that Mia had sketched and described for us." Shelbi looked up and smiled.

Griffin, Cable, and Maggie looked at the frames, back at Shelbi, and back to the frames as if watching a tennis game in slow motion.

"Wow," said Griffin as he looked at Mia's sketch. "Well done. You did better than we managed. Is this roughly to scale?"

"Yes," answered Mia. "I had my notes with dimensions and the frames are about right and the blanket represents the van."

Brent continued, "We concluded that it would be best if we did not ride across the lake inside a metal coffin in case it goes down, so we plan to stand along the sides of the van and can adjust our positions to change the balance and center of gravity."

Shelbi walked over to the raft and described, "The dining tables out front have pretty heavy-duty boards that are over 3 meters long and we want to disassemble them to make 2 wide ramps that the van would park on and we would stand on. We don't need a full platform. Our stuff goes in the van and we stand on the outside like Brent said."

"Oh, my gosh, in all the activity I forgot to make lunch," said Shelbi.

"Then our propulsion system would go here, between the 2 rows of logs," Griffin said as he gestured and moved behind the prototype. "The logs should provide some direction stabilization like a twin-hull catamaran. We just need a thrust vector."

"I have an idea," said Griffin. "I am going to look for pumps at the water ride." He started out the door, Abby and Cable looked at each other and quickly followed.

"I kept thinking of this as a race like my car, Solar Cup, the Baja Racer, but we just need to get across the lake. It doesn't have to be fast, but it must be reliable and light. We need less pressure in the front and more pressure in the back, a pressure differential." Griffin was talking like no one was really there, he was processing out loud, something his companions were used to. "If we find a pump, we can draw water from the bow and then discharge to the stern. When I was researching those cool water jet packs, I found out that there is almost no difference whether we discharge our water stream underwater or above. It is all about pressure and velocity, so it only works if we have a good pump. Our best chance is at the remote locations on the log ride that have to use a water stream to move the logs."

"So, your plan is to look in the upper channels of the log ride and see if they use remote pumps and then see if they are compatible with our small generator?" asked Cable.

"That could work," said Abby. "There! A ladder up near the upper channel through the trees. We can either climb the log ramp or the ladder."

"Let's try the ramp," said Cable. "I've had enough falling and crashing this week."

They climbed until they reached the top. Griffin stepped over the overgrown plants to the small attendant platform off to the side of the channel and stepped out onto the ladder that disappeared into the trees.

"I see hoses coming up from the loading zone and no pumps hanging from the hoses. I only see valves. I guess this makes sense because all the water flows downhill and had to be pumped back up to the top somehow. The pumps would have to be huge to drive the water up this hill, so this probably won't work."

"I wonder if there are any local pumps to just assist along the way," said Cable. "It makes sense that the big hoses and pumps would have to be at the start to get the water up the hill, but maybe there are small pumps that boost the flow. Let's look further along the channel."

The channel was mostly empty except for the puddles from the recent rains making the walk treacherous and wet. After traversing several ups and downs they continued to only find hoses and valves but no pumps.

"Maybe we are thinking too big, coming to the log ride," said Abby. "Can we think of anywhere else that would have smaller pumps and not hydraulic pumps because those make pressure but not enough flow rate? Let's head back. Ladder or ramp?"

"There is a ladder right here and we are lower now," said Griffin. "I can't see the bottom because of the trees, but what could go wrong?"

"Oh, I don't know," said Cable. "The ladder breaking as we climb down. Falling to our death. The ladder ending before it gets to the ground. Sure, let's try it."

Griffin had already swung his legs over the rail and was starting down the ladder and disappeared in a thrashing of leaves and branches. Abby followed and just as Cable was about to start down, he heard Griffin call out that he was down.

They reached the bottom and brushed bits of leaves off each other's faces and shoulders and picked a few out of each other's hair.

"That was fun," said Griffin. "Where else can you think that there would be a pump in this park?"

"Fountains," Abby paused. "Fountains, like the one that is at the entrance. That must have a pretty strong pump, it's over 5 meters tall."

"You're right. We have walked by it a dozen times, but since it's not running, it looks like just a big statue surrounded by weeds," said Cable.

"Let's go find the pump," said Abby as they started walking down the hill. "Griff, what do you think about the bed frame idea?"

"I like it. It uses strong frames, so it doesn't require welding and they seem like the right size. I like the ramp idea and, as much as I like being in cars, I agree that we should be outside this one for the voyage across the lake."

They came around the road to the entrance of the park and could see the fountain tower out of the tiled pool. Plants of all types sprang out of the pool and vines trailed over the wall.

"The pump should be pretty close to the fountain but might be behind a wall to hide the sound," said Griffin.

"There is a shed just inside the fence of the blue coaster," said Abby.

"Nah, that's just the equipment cage for the coaster motor," said Cable. "That is where I got the fan from."

"No, that little structure that is disguised as the fishing shack," said Griffin.

"I know the way into that fence from behind the Cool Zone," said Cable as he led the way around the derelict building and the overgrown plants. He grabbed the shovel that he had leaned against the back wall. The back of the shack had a padlock, but the shovel quickly removed the hasp.

"That is quite a pump," said Griffin. "Let's see if we can find a power rating to see if it will work with our generator. There is a spec plate on it."

230V, 17.6 A @ 19,740 GPH @ 12 ft.

"That is a big one, so we need at least 15 amp but 20 is better. 230 times 17.6 is about 4000 Watts. What was the generator?" asked Cable.

"I think it was only 2500, but worth a try," said Griffin. "We should fuel it up and bring it down here and connect it to see if the pump is seized. Is there enough water in the fountain to turn this on?"

"Let's go see on our way back to DreamLand," said Abby drearily and a hint of sarcasm on the word 'dream.'

They wound their way around the Cool Zone and peered over the fountain wall through the plants and vines.

"There is water but not sure if there is trash or dirt that will get sucked in. Hopefully, the filter will catch the bad stuff," said Griffin as they started their walk back up the hill. They were quiet for a few minutes as they walked.

"Well, where are we at for the day?" asked Cable. "The bike is running, we have a prototype frame concept, we have a fan but no way to spin it and found a pump that might work." He paused. "We also have our lives, running water, enough food, and each other."

"Has anyone done the math about how much food we have and how long we think it will take to get everything built to get across the lake?" asked Abby.

"Not really," replied Griffin. "I've just seen that we have lots of cans of food and bags of rice, but I haven't figured out the math. Since we are the primary propulsion team, what do we think about how soon we can get something running?"

Abby replied, "I think we could get something running in a couple of days. If the other team can work on the frame and we focus on the propulsion it might be a good division of labor. We need to figure a way to get those logs moved so they can start working."

"How about we move the 4 we need for the raft right to the water so we only need to do that once and move one to DreamLand so they can measure and prototype?" suggested Griffin.

"Do you think we can use dollies or just use the van?" asked Abby.

"I bet those logs weigh a few hundred pounds each, probably safer to use the van," said Cable.

They were just coming around the corner of the theater and could see DreamLand and several people were working in the outdoor dining area.

"What are they up to?" asked Abby.

"They are taking apart the tables, cool," said Cable.

"How are things going, Maggie," called Griffin.

"Great, we decided to start working on the ramps since we had the socket set. We have removed 6 of the 8 boards that we need, and things are coming together well."

"That sounds better than our day," said Abby. "We found one pump that is a bit more powerful than we can run, have a motorcycle that we can't figure out how to use to drive a propeller, and have a fan that we can't mount to anything."

Cody poked his head outside and announced, "Dinner is ready."

"Where is Shelbi?" asked Cable.

"She has moved from hospitality to engineering," joked Brent.

Dinner was the unremarkable mixture of rice and canned vegetables, but the energy of the space was buzzing with excitement over the recent successes in raft structure.

"We were thinking of moving 4 logs to the shore and bringing 1 over here so you could prototype," said Griffin. "Also, it seems like we are starting to form some teams. Cable, Abby, and I are working on propulsion, but we welcome any help. Maggie? Brent, Shelbi, Cody, and Mia are working on the structure, right?"

"I would like to work with you guys on propulsion," said Maggie.

"Maybe I can help by doing the cooking from now," said Sterling. "Your brains are better suited for getting us out of here. The least I can do is cook for you."

"Alright, so let's do this!" exclaimed Cable.

The group finished their food and gathered around the campfire, silently staring into the fire as the flames curled and puffed. The daily breeze that blows down their mountain and out over the lake was tapering to occasional swish.

"I charged my phone today and have some music that speaks to me right now. Do you mind if I play it?" asked Mia.

"Please do," said Shelbi. "I miss music. I had been pretty depressed lately but working on the raft structure has been a real boost."

"I've never shared this with anyone. I was abused as a kid. This time with you," Mia paused and everyone looked at her with kind eyes. "Has made me stronger. We are warriors. Thank you for believing in me, in us. 'This is ME'"

The group leaned in to hear the phone and recognized the tune.

I am not a stranger to the dark
Hide away, they say
'Cause we don't want your broken parts
I've learned to be ashamed of all my scars...

Shelbi's eyes glistened and she started to sing softly. Mia had closed her eyes, but it did not hold back her tears.

Another round of bullets hits my skin
Well, fire away 'cause today, I won't let the shame sink in
We are bursting through the barricades and
Reaching for the sun (we are warriors)
Yeah, that's what we've become

I won't let them break me down to dust

I know that there's a place for us

For we are glorious

When the song ended the world went still. The whole group gathered in a single hug, even Sterling, standing, with arms around shoulders.

"We are going to be ok. Like Watney said, 'We are going to work the problem, science the snot out of this,' and we will get out and get back home," said Cable.

CHAPTER 21 – PLUMBING

Science is beautiful when it makes simple explanations of phenomena or connections between different observations. Examples include the double helix in biology and the fundamental equations of physics. - Stephen Hawking

Griffin and Cable were up early to get the van and move logs.

"We'll be back with the van in a little while so we need everyone who can help meet us over at the log ride," said Griffin as he and Cable left.

"Is there anything else we ought to do while we are driving around?" asked Cable.

"Hit the Starbucks drive-thru?" joked Griffin.

"I wish," said Cable.

Griffin opened the driver's door and looked behind the seat at the batteries.

"Let's see," he started. "We have to connect the positive cable to the positive rail and then do the ignition wires."

He bent the cable to contact the rail and was rewarded with a blue spark, so he tightened the lug. Flipping the seat back and sitting down he looked at the ignition wires.

"These weren't quite color order, so I think they were yellow for gauges, red for fuel pump, then orange to start," said Griffin as if to remind himself.

"Here we go. Yellow, red……. And orange."

The engine rattled to life. Griffin pressed the clutch and found first gear. Easing the clutch out, the van lurched forward, and he guided it around the warehouse and around the park to the log ride. As he passed DreamLand, he found the button for the horn and then pulled up to the log ride just as Cody was using a long pipe to force the gate open to get closer to the boathouse. Griffin found reverse and eased the clutch out again, but this time the van shook and popped and then jerked backward up to the boathouse where he disconnected the wires, set the brake, and then breathed and looked at Cable.

"Not bad, only 4 more times," joked Cable.

"I think the best logs will be the ones that have been under the boathouse roof since they are not full of water or damaged by the sun," said Cody. "Let's get the best 5 from back here."

The rest of the group, who could help, was arriving as Griffin opened the back of the van. Mia and Cody were each carrying a dolly.

"Let's set these right next to the first log and see if we can roll it most of the way to the van," suggested Cody.

With 3 people on each side, they lifted the first log and set it on the dollies. Guiding it carefully, each had a hand on it as it bumped along to the van. Each took their positions and heaved the log into the van, with only a bit of space to spare on the sides. The log hung out of the back, so Griffin used a wire to hold the doors against the end of the log. 3 people got into the log and 3 squeezed into the front for the ride down to the shore.

Griffin started up the van and it coasted into first gear easily on the way downhill. As they reached the water, Griffin turned the van around and backed toward the pier but at the last moment, he turned to the space between the pier and the main section of the plane.

Griffin explained, "I was thinking that we could build it on the pier but realized that it would be difficult to launch from up there, and this way we can use the end of the pier as an anchor point to pull the raft into the water. Let's set these as close to the water as we think is safe because it will just be getting bigger and heavier as we build."

The 6 kids exited and carried the log across the rocky beach until it nearly touched the lapping water's edge. They loaded up and drove back up the hill for the next one. This process was repeated until they got the 5th log, which they transported right to the doors of the DreamLand building main entrance. Everyone was so excited to have a log in their workspace they forgot what teams they were working in and moved a couple bedframes to see if they would fit as expected. Mia's drawings were spot-on, and one frame fit near the rear and the other appeared would bridge the gap from the front log to rear log.

"You realize that if use our bedframes we have no place to sleep," said Brent.

"There are still some up in the bunkhouse, right?" asked Mia.

"While we have the van out, Cable and I will move 3 frames down to the pier," said Griffin as he and Cable dashed out the door.

The 3 frames fit, standing on edge and hanging out the back of the van. Arriving at the shore, they set the frames down in their approximate locations on the logs and then high-fived each other.

"This might just work," said Cable. "I'm hungry. Let's eat."

Arriving at DreamLand, Sterling was just serving up soup and everyone was busy talking about raft designs.

"This is a nice change of pace," said Brent. "The soup is so good, Sterling. We are excited to have you in the kitchen. Thanks."

"We still only have the same 5 ingredients," joked Sterling.

Although it was the same 5 ingredients, just being something different seemed to bring a smile to everyone's face as they ate.

"By the way, could you transport the 6 heavy boards to the shore after lunch? That is the last of the big stuff we need for the raft."

"Sure," replied Griffin. "Is there anything else we need to do with the van?"

"We need to move the generator down to test the pump," answered Cable.

"Right. Let's go," said Griffin.

They loaded the boards in the van and then went to the shed to get the generator.

"3500 Watts!" exclaimed Cable. "That helps. This is going to take two of us to lift it in the van."

They shook it and it was about half full. Griffin suggested that they top it off with kerosene so that they could have a full tank of a mixed fuel that might run better than pure kerosene.

"While we have the van and have to get the generator near that pump, how about we 'open' the gate near the pump shack using the van?" suggested Cable.

"I'm game," said Griffin as he pulled the van around the fountain, smashing through the brush and brought the bumper up to the wood gate. The stick shift made this operation a bit more abrupt so the contact with the gate was harder than he intended, but the end result was achieved.

"Well, that happened," laughed Cable.

Griffin jerked the shifter into reverse and maneuvered the van out into the walkway to turn around and then backed over the trampled brush and gate. The back of the van and the generator were only a few feet from the pump shack now, so they eased the generator to the ground and connected an extension cord to the generator, but not the pump yet.

"Let's start this up and then we will connect the pump. One thing at a time," said Griffin as he switched on the fuel, power, and choke then pulled the cord. After several pulls, the motor sputtered and coughed. He adjusted the choke and gave another pull to which they were rewarded with a fairly smooth *poppity-pop* rhythm of exhaust.

"You watch the top of the fountain and I will watch the pump and will be ready to pull the plug if something goes wrong," said Griffin.

They got in their places, Cable on top of the shack for a better view of the fountain over the grasses, and Griffin connected the cords. The generator lugged a bit, but kept running, and did not pop a breaker. The pump squealed for a while and then got quieter.

"Water! Water is coming out on top!" exclaimed Cable.

Griffin pulled the plug.

"Well, we have a pump if we can get it out of here," said Cable. "The inlet side is just hose clamped, but the outlet is glued."

"Makes sense, on the high-pressure side," replied Griffin. "Can you get a saw in there?"

"Better yet, there is a coupling that we can disassemble. We need to figure out what hose we can use for the raft. It's not like we have a Home Depot with fittings and adapters."

"Oh," said Griffin. "We just might. There was a maintenance shed behind the boathouse I saw when we were loading logs. We were so focused on logs, but I bet they keep plumbing repair things up there."

After an hour of dropping off boards, returning the generator to the shed, grabbing wrenches and screwdrivers, they drove back to extract the pump.

"I think that coupling is about 3 inch and I remember that some of the hoses in the upper log ride were about the same size," noted Griffin. "If nothing else we might just cut some hose off of the ride."

"Did you say that we get the same thrust whether the water is discharged above or below the water?" asked Cable. "That seems strange that pushing against water or air would be the same."

"It's not the fact that we are pushing against anything," said Griffin. "It is the Newton law thing about momentum. The fact that we are discharging the mass of the water at a velocity is what creates the thrust. Hmm, I have to think about this. We need to think about the mass flow rate. A nozzle will increase the speed of the water and therefore might increase the momentum as long as we do not decrease the amount of water."

"This 3" discharge will allow a lot of flow," started Cable. "Hey, there were nozzles up on the log channel! Maybe that hike up the ramp was not wasted."

They arrived at the log ride and opened the back of the van to inspect the pipe sizes and fittings. They were greeted by Maggie and Abby.

"We don't want you to have all the fun," said Abby. "We heard you driving back up the hill. What have you found?"

"The pump ran and pumped water to the fountain and did not kill the generator," said Cable. "Probably because we were only lifting the water a few meters. Ah, Griff, that is what we will have to be careful about. If we restrict the water too much through a nozzle, we could create more backpressure and draw too much power from the generator. It's easy enough to test."

"I like what I am hearing," said Maggie. "The generator is big enough to drive the pump and you are thinking nozzles. What are you looking for up here?"

"The plumbing section of our lovely DreamLand," quipped Cable. "Come with us. See the inlet and outlet of this pump are about 3" and we figure we need a way to draw water from the front of the raft and discharge from the stern, so we need about 6 meters of hose or pipe."

While Cable was talking, Griffin had climbed the fence and was looking for nozzles in the channels. Leaping from channel edge to edge and hanging over the sides, he made his way through the lower part of the ride. Cable, Maggie, and Abby were looking at fittings, hoses, wires and a bunch of miscellaneous materials that did not seem to match the construction of this ride.

"Paper towels," said Maggie.

"Disposable rain jackets," replied Abby.

"Fuses, colored light bulbs, and a horse's head," Cable nonchalantly added.

"What?!" exclaimed Abby and Maggie together.

"From the carousel," replied Cable.

"What's this?" asked Maggie. "Can you help me unfold it?"

"It's two old flags for the entrance, DreamLand. I thought that was just the name of our main hall, but that appears to be the name of the park. What a dream it is. This could be handy since it is large and like a rubberized canvas. I will throw it in the van," said Cable as he ran his hand across it.

"I found nozzles," yelled Griffin from some invisible place beyond the bushes. Suddenly his curly hair popped up from behind a channel. "I need a saw and some hose clamps, and I think this will fit our pump. Any luck finding hose?"

"There is a spool of the same size back behind the shed," said Abby as she emerged through the plants. "I just found it. We need something like a hack saw for this stuff."

"If we are all done moving the big stuff, I will take the van back to the shed and walk back with a hack saw," said Griffin.

"Sounds good," replied Abby. "We will assemble the fittings we will need."

Abby, Cable, and Maggie dug through bins and looked over disorganized workbenches for fittings and other items that seemed useful and began to assemble a mock-up of a jet system on the ground.

"I remember from the Solar Cup project that the biggest impact on movement through a fluid is the total wetted area, displacement, and disturbances. All protrusions create vortices that rob power. The fact that we are trying to propel 4 logs through water with a few thousand kilos of displacement is not ideal. We need to hold the front logs as close to the rear ones as possible and it would be great to cover the gap between them. We should minimize the other protrusions into the water, so our water intake should be out of the flow, maybe in front of one of the lead logs. Then the hose needs to run to the pump. The inlet of the pump was on the end and the outlet pointed up, but we can probably turn it on its side."

"The pump is heavy," said Maggie. "But so is the generator. Seems like we should either put both inside the van or on either side to maintain balance."

"And they should be as low as possible," added Abby.

Maggie continued, "The lowest center of gravity would be to set them on the raft planks. How about between the sets of van wheels? They would be low and balanced. Even though they are spread apart the net c of g would be the equivalent of a single mass at the center of the van but as low as the deck."

"Listen to you," admired Cable. "You have been sitting in these classes taking notes, acing tests, and you are an engineering powerhouse hiding in plain sight."

Maggie blushed a bit. "Anyway. Does my math check out?"

"Yes, I agree," said Cable. "This means we need the hose to come up at the front and maybe run under the van, so we don't trip over it, then go through the pump, and back under the van to the center stern. Let's lay that out."

By the time Griffin had returned and brought Cody and Mia back with him, there was a preliminary layout of fittings on the ground. The propulsion team presented their ideas and the observations about optimizing the raft for flow dynamics. Griffin measured off about 3.5 meters of hose and cut it with the saw, and then a second one of the same length. The group worked with the pieces and called for some shorter pieces and Griffin delivered.

"Glue!" said Cable, who was rummaging through the bins in the shed.

Cable opened the can and then closed it with a smile on his face. "We can't really glue anything until we fit-check everything on the raft and van in place, but we have what we need. We can leave the hoses long and assemble it all now and then cut and glue at the raft."

The group completed two sections, one that would point down in front of the lead log and run to the axial input, and the second section that would arc under the van and direct its flow through the nozzle that Griffin scavenged from the ride. They carried the two thick snakes back to DreamLand to see how it lined up with the bedframe mockup.

Brent and Shelbi had been busy trying out different lashing methods and were proud to present their design to the group. Sterling had made another meal, this time browning the rice with the vegetables in a skillet.

"How did you fry this up so nice," asked Mia.

"I found a full container of vegetable oil, same containers you have been working with here in the hall," said Sterling. "It was still sealed and smelled right. Even though I cannot read the markings on the side, there was a picture of a corncob on the container of golden clear oil."

"This is delicious. Thank you, Sterling," said Cable.

"We had a productive day," remarked Griffin.

"We have moved all our raft materials, found a pump, plumbed a water jet," agreed Cable.

Shelbi added, "I want to take our lashing materials to the shore tomorrow and start assembling the raft."

CHAPTER 22 – WILL IT FLOAT

Every once in a while, a new technology, an old problem, and a big idea turn into an innovation. - Dean Kamen

The morning sun was accompanied by the typical breeze from the mountain above. Everyone ate quickly and the structure group had gathered around the bedframes. During the prototyping stage, they had left the bedframes in their mock-up positions and just put the blankets on them and slept in them as they were arranged. Shelbi's bed happened to be the one in the middle now that the raft had been reduced to 3 frames and 4 logs.

"We need to take our wire and cord," began Shelbi. "The logs, carboys, and planks are already at the shore. Mia, can we get the dimensions of the van?"

"I have my notebook," said Mia.

"Anything else?" asked Shelbi as she paused. "Let's go." She grabbed her arm crutch off of the bed and headed for the door.

"It's less steep if you go out the west side and curve around past the Cool Zone," said Cable who realized that Shelbi had only seen part of the park so far.

The group worked their way down the hill.

Cody noted, "The grasses are starting to be cleared from the road as we have driven around, a bit easier than a week ago."

"But the Cool Zone is just as creepy as the first day," added Mia.

"One thing that we should think about is how we are going to load the van on the raft and then get the raft off the ground," said Shelbi. "I think the raft should be floating when we drive onto it, otherwise, we will not be able to drag it on the rocks."

Cody noted, "Let's set a goal to have the whole raft tied together today and maybe we can drag it out to the end of the pier to see how it floats. Since there are only 4 of us out here, let's move the first 2 logs into shallow water, then add 1 bedframe and push it out and add the next 2 logs. We can keep it along the pier, so we have easy access."

They were able to lift and drag each log to the water and the first bedframe dropped right into the hulls as they had hoped. By lashing the corner posts to the interior rails of the logs it became rigid and secure. They dragged the next two logs to the water and pushed the raft out a bit more. Even when the rear logs were pushed tight to the forward logs the bedframe would not quite reach from one opening to another. Just about this time, Maggie and Cable appeared carrying a box.

"Lunch anyone?" announced Cable.

"Yes, that would be great, especially not having to walk back up the hill," said Shelbi.

"We just ran into a snag," said Cody. "The bed frame won't quite reach across the span from the front log to the rear one."

"Can you trim off anything from the logs?" asked Cable. "That would be easier than stretching the frames, right?"

"The logs are cast fiberglass," said Mia.

"But they have bumpers," added Cody.

"If we can rip those off then they will fit," said Shelbi. "Maybe we want to leave one set on to provide some protection between the two."

"I will go get you the prybars," said Cable as he stood to go. Maggie joined him as they walked back to the shed.

"OK," said Shelbi. "Let's assume that will solve that problem. In the meantime, we can lash the rear frame, so these logs don't float away."

"Float away," said Mia. "Have you seen that these logs have been trying to float away all day? I hadn't noticed it, but this breeze normally blows across the lake, doesn't it? I wonder if we could use sail power."

"It's not as reliable, but it might work," said Cody.

About the time they had the rear frame attached, Cable returned with the prybars. Not content to just hand off all the fun, Cable climbed onto the frame and along the log until he could jamb one bar between the fiberglass and the bumper. He pushed and handed the other bar to Cody who had joined him. Cody saw the opening and pushed his bar into the narrow space created by Cable's bar. Working together, they moved their pair of dissecting forces along the bumper until it popped off. They slid the logs together and the frame fit with almost no room to spare.

"Perfect fit. Aren't you supposed to be working on propulsion somewhere?" joked Shelbi.

"Ya, but this looked fun," replied Cable. "Griffin is working on adapting the fittings of the pump, sort of a one-person job right now. Maggie and I have recruited Brent to help us make some tall paddles that we can use to push off the bottom with one end and paddle and steer. I need to find something that will make a good paddle blade to attach to our tall poles."

"How about those metal signs," Mia said as she pointed near the ticket booths. "They have holes and could be bent into blades around poles."

"Perfect. Thanks. I will grab them on my way. See you later. Dinner will be when the sun hits the ridge, OK?"

The group pried off the other bumper and finished lashing all the frames down. The planks attached just as they hoped and were quite secure, reaching about half a meter in front and behind the log assemblies. As they checked the dimensions of the van wheelbase, they were finding that the wheels and planks were directly over the inner handrails.

"This load path looks really good," remarked Shelbi, who had sat down on the pier and could help hold, lash, and direct without falling into the water. "The load from the wheels will rest on the planks that are in contact with the frames and the logs, so nothing is really in bending. I am excited to put the van up onto this."

"Let's float it around the pier first," said Cody.

"I suppose," said Shelbi. "Aren't we about ready?"

"I am making a few dock lines," said Mia. "Here you go. I'll tie one to the stern frame."

After attaching the dock lines, the group walked the raft out to the end of the pier and tied it off to the cleats. Cody jumped out onto the planks and bounced as much as he could, but the raft was stable. Mia joined Cody on the left plank and could not get the raft to ripple more than the lake waves were contributing. As they stood there, they saw that Shelbi was looking past them. They turned around and were all looking at the ragged end of the plane that was just west of their location, close enough to see the tatters of fabric and wires blowing in the breeze.

"This looks really great," said Shelbi as she came back to the current operation. "I wonder what it does when we drive a van on top of it. Let's pull it back as close to shore as we can, tie it off and head back to camp. The sun has almost reached the ridge."

The structures group was quite excited about their progress for the day and were busy chatting as they walked up past the Cool Zone and turned into their weedy path to DreamLand.

"Hey, how did it go?" called Cable from the outdoor dining pavilion where he and Brent were forming paddles.

"It floats," said Cody in his manner-of-fact way.

"It was remarkably stable," continued Shelbi. Cody and Mia were jumping around on it and it responded more to the lake waves than it did to their bouncing. We should probably test it with the van soon. We realized we need a couple more planks to get the van from the shore to the raft and still have the raft floating, so we don't ground it out."

Griffin came outside and said, "Sounds like you have a raft. Are you about ready to fit a pump system onto it?"

"Yes," confirmed Shelbi. "I think the only thing remaining is to add more removable driving planks and we can put everything on. We did not use any of the carboy containers yet since the lashings and load paths worked out so well. We really need to see how low this sits when fully loaded with the van and the 9 of us."

"I have been thinking about something," said Griffin. "Where are we headed? I mean we have a raft and a van but if we come ashore on a rocky beach, or cliff, or dense forest it won't matter that we made it to the other side of the lake."

Sterling had been standing in the doorway, "On that note, dinner is ready."

As they served up food, Cable said, "We have 3 good paddles that can be turned around and used as push poles. We should be able to direct ourselves a bit with the paddles used as rudders, but we have to hope we can see some pier as we're crossing so we know what to aim for."

"I was thinking about center of gravity," said Maggie. "What if we loaded the pump and generator down in the logs? It is the same net load, but it is even lower and might stabilize the raft."

"Hmm, the pump is no problem, but I don't know if we want to be generating 230 volts below the splash level," said Cable. "Sort of reminds me of running 200 Amps in the Solar Cup boat, just a few centimeters behind my head."

"You lived," joked Griffin. "We will do the load test tomorrow and see what we see."

"It's been 10 days since we crashed. I am going to do laundry tomorrow so if you have anything, leave it on the end of the counter in the morning," said Sterling.

CHAPTER 23 – LOAD IT UP

The five essential entrepreneurial skills for success: Concentration, Discrimination, Organization, Innovation and Communication. - Harold S. Geneen

The morning sun streaked across the dining hall-turned bedroom. The scent of breakfast lingered in the air. Everyone had eaten and was piling up laundry items on the counter.

"Today is a big day, all-hands-on-deck," said Griffin.

"If you are driving the van, is there any way you could pick me up for the load test?" asked Brent.

"Since you have been less of a jerk lately and you asked nicely, I am happy to pick you up," laughed Griffin.

Everyone chuckled and Brent actually smiled.

The group started moving to the shore, Griffin started the van right up and drove to pick up Brent and Shelbi. Instead of staying on the ring road, he plowed through the grasses of the interior lane and pulled up right in the dining pavilion where they were waiting. Griffin loaded 4 more planks in the back after moving the generator and pump.

"I appreciate this," said Brent. "I have been missing being a part of the structure crew."

"Sure. No problem," said Griffin.

They pulled the van up right behind the raft as the crew was moving it out into deeper water. Griffin watched as there was discussion and pointing.

"One of the logs has a lot of water in it," said Maggie. "Unfortunately, it is the one in the front, farthest from the pier."

"OK," said Griffin. "We need to get one more, either from the boathouse or DreamLand. I think I can drive closer to the ones in the boathouse, but we need all the heavy lifters."

Brent traded places with the others and was left on the pier with Shelbi. The pump, generator, and planks were unloaded, and the van disappeared up the road.

"I haven't had a good bath in a while," said Brent and he pulled off his shoes, shirt, and jeans and waded into the lake alongside the logs. He shivered as he entered the water, turning his face to the warm sun, then splashed the fresh water on his arms and chest as if to prepare himself for the swim. He started untying the cords and was about ready to lift the frame off when the van returned.

"Whatcha doin?" asked Cable. "We go lift a heavy log into the van and you're at the beach for a swim."

"I figured I could use a bath and the water takes the load off of my knee," replied Brent. "And I untied all the lashings, so we are ready to swap it out. See if you can climb out on the rear log and lift the joining frame. I think I can lift the front frame and push the log out."

"OK, hold on. We will bring the new log down first so we can swap it."

The crew slid the log out of the van and carried it to the water. Mia attached a cord to it and handed it to Cable who climbed his way across the frames and planks and stood in the rear log to lift the frame. He tied off the new log to his log and grabbed the frame.

"Go."

Both frames were lifted, and Brent pushed the log free of the frames. Cable pulled on the cord and swung the new log around to Brent. He had to lift the frame a little higher since this log was sitting higher in the water, but it dropped right in. Cable's frame was a bit tougher with the tight fit, but luckily the boat that leaked was the one that still had its bumper.

"Let's get these all lashed and do our test," said Brent. "I will do all the ones out on the outside if someone can do the ones near the plank."

Planks and frames were getting tied down, generator and pump moved to the pier and the ramps were getting attached to the rear planks.

"This is going to be interesting," said Griffin. "Check the physics with me, OK? As we drive this on, won't we get a bit of a horizontal force and suddenly half the weight of the van, including the engine, will be on the first edge of the raft. I think we need to tie the raft to shore so it does not squirt out in front of us. We also need to somehow support the back edge until the van gets centered. We really don't want to drop the van into the lake or sink our raft today."

Maggie thought and replied, "I think you are right, and it cannot hurt to do either one. To support the raft, we need a way that we can remove the support after loading so we need a way to collapse or pull something out."

"How about levers," said Cable. "Like when we lifted up Mr. Alpin's truck. We could have levers holding up the raft and as soon as we are ready, we can remove the weight on the lever to remove them."

"Oh, Mr. Alpin," said Shelbi. "I miss having his input on stuff like this. I almost miss his puns. I like the lever idea. Can we use two of the planks?"

Cable and Cody found some large rocks and rolled them into place to act at the fulcrums for the two levers. Meanwhile, Mia was making more dock lines and staked the raft in place.

"OK," said Griffin. "Let's take this really slowly and if anyone sees this going sideways you need to yell so I can back up."

Everyone took positions to observe. Abby stood in the middle of the raft to direct Griffin up the ramps. Griffin started the engine, put it in first gear, but kept the clutch in while he rolled slowly as Abby provided direction. Once his tires were in contact and got the thumbs up, Abby backed up to the front of the raft. Griffin slowly let the clutch out and the front tires began their narrow traverse. The back tires had to climb the ramps before the front tires dropped onto the wider planks. At the bounce, Griffin quickly clutched and hit the brakes.

"You are OK, the front tires just dropped onto the planks. You are centered and good to go," reassured Maggie, who was on the pier right outside Griffin's window.

Griffin eased the clutch out again and the rear tires crawled along the ramps. The raft was starting to dip in the front, but not alarmingly so he still had thumbs up from Abby. The rear tires were approaching the end of the ramps, so Maggie warned him this time.

"Less than a meter to go," yelled Abby and repeated by Maggie.

Abby crossed her arms and Griffin clutched, braked, and froze. Cable and Cody lowered the long levers and the raft settled into a comfortable level. "We are floating!" yelled Cable. "Are you going to shut off the engine, Griff?"

"I don't know yet," he replied. "I don't want it to stall out here. I will set the parking brake and put it in neutral and everyone get on board for the test.

"Don't forget the generator and pump," said Maggie, who was standing next to both.

Griffin set the brake, and everyone loaded the gear on and then jumped on board.

"Is that everything?" asked Griffin.

"Everyone except Sterling, but she is lighter than me," said Maggie. "We made a raft that holds a van and 8 people. We did it. We did it." She wiped a tear from her cheek. "How does everything look on the other side?"

"Good," replied Cable. The waves are making things go up and down a bit, but it looks pretty stable. One thing that I would recommend is that we strap down each wheel with those heavy-duty ratchet straps, so we don't have any movement while in transit. I also think we should leave first thing in the morning before the breeze picks up and the waves get stronger."

"Good point," said Abby. "OK, let's put Griff out of his misery and back this thing off. Everybody get off the raft. Griff, you might have a bit of a bump to get the back tires over the ramp boards. Cable and Cody, support the levers. Everyone ready?"

Abby gave Griffin a thumbs up but followed up with, "Don't forget to use reverse!"

"Thanks for the reminder," he replied as he clutched, removed the parking brake, and found what he hoped was reverse. To be sure he just let the clutch out enough to make sure it was going the right way. He let out the clutch again and felt the rear wheel hop up onto the planks. Holding the steering straight he continued to back down the ramps but nearly came off with the front tires, but by that time the van was on firm ground and it did not matter.

"I have seen videos of these vans crossing streams in Russia and all over the world. No problem," said Griffin. "How about we use two boards for each ramp like the planks next time," said Abby.

"No complaints there," replied Griffin. "Let's go work on the pump. Who wants a ride?"

Griffin, Cable, Abby, and Maggie loaded the generator and pump in the van, and all went to work on the propulsion system, and they dropped Brent off on the way.

The others stayed to add lashings for the next voyage. Cody checked the logs, and none had any water in the bottom.

"Is there anything that we need to fix or improve for the real journey?" asked Cody.

"Just the double-wide ramps and the wheel straps," replied Shelbi. "And maybe beef up our lashings from the top of the planks through the frames and down to the handrails inside the logs. We can even use the straps to go from the wheels all the way to the handrails so that we stabilize the whole load path."

Mia, Cody, and Shelbi continued to strap things down and moved the levers further onto shore. The wind had increased, and it was getting cold, so as soon as they had things ready, they returned to camp.

The propulsion team members were joining hoses and fittings to the pump.

Abby proposed, "We should test this out tomorrow just to make sure that the generator can drive this pump with the hoses and nozzle. I'm just not sure whether we try in on the raft and possibly float away or just test it on the pier."

"Let's do the pier test first and then see about the raft," replied Cable. "We definitely want to run it on the raft before we have a van and 9 people on there."

"That's true," confirmed Maggie. "If we put it on the raft, we can also work out our final hose lengths and glue things up."

Griffin noted, "Oh, we can't run the nozzle until we glue, and we can't glue until we fit check everything, so we are definitely testing on the raft tomorrow. There is the super long cable that we found that we can connect to the raft and if something goes really wrong, we can pull ourselves back in."

"This wind is picking up," said Maggie. "Let's go back to camp."

"Now that you mention that long cable, I am going to run it down to the raft on my way back. I will meet you back at DreamLand," said Cable.

As they arrived at camp all the clean clothes were strung up on the lighting cables under the pavilion, dry and fresh.

"This is amazing, Sterling," remarked Maggie. "Thanks so much."

"I don't know what I will do with such clean clothes," said Cody.

"We won't be able to tell when you are coming anymore," joked Abby.

"Dinner will be ready in a while," said Sterling. "You are back earlier than usual. You can get cleaned up. Did you know that if you use the staff shower down the hall that the water is warm for the first minute or so?"

"What!" exclaimed Mia. "There is a shower? I have been using the bathrooms out by the pavilion and there are no showers."

"I had my bath today, so I am all good," said Brent. "I think the cold water helped my knee too."

Mia was already running down the hall with a handful of clean clothes, and everyone chuckled, wishing they had moved as fast.

The rest of the group was washing up and resting when Mia emerged, sparkling clean.

"That was amazing," said Mia. "And you are right, the first minute was less cold. I am clean and happy."

About this time, Cable entered, "That wind is picking up out there, glad we are not trying to sail across right now."

A while later, Sterling announced dinner. "You seemed to like the fried rice, so I worked with that theme tonight. Fried rice patties."

"I've never heard of those," said Cable.

"Neither have I," admitted Sterling. "We have rice and water and oil and some spices, so I made rice and added a bit more water and made patties then fried them like burgers. When life gives you rice, make anything you can out of it."

"This is great, Sterling," said Mia. "I thought I had rice every way possible but this is great."

"I thought I have had everything fried that existed, but never had this," said Abby. "My mom's side is from the south so she would make fried chicken, fried okra, fried apples, fried Johnnycake."

"I've never met your mom," said Maggie. "Is she African American?"

"Yep, but she died when I was 7 so it has just been me and my dad for the last 10 years, but I remember those foods."

"I'm so sorry," said Maggie, feeling awkward for bringing it up.

"No worries, my dad is awesome, and he has taught me some great things and not just welding. I also know how to box too, so don't mess with me," Abby joked, easing the tension.

Every last rice patty was gone, and Cable even pinched the last bits out of the pan. The group sat around talking for a while as it got dark and the wind rattled the windows. The building moaned and shuttered as the students tried to fall asleep.

CHAPTER 24 — LOST

The only way you survive is you continuously transform into something else. It's this idea of continuous transformation that makes you an innovation company. - Ginni Rometty

The air was eerily still when Griffin first opened his eyes in the early morning light. He quietly got up and looked outside to see new branches littering the walkways. The air smelled of crushed foliage. Having a sinking feeling about the raft, he quietly exited and grabbed a bike for a quick trip to the shore. As he rounded the corner by Cool Zone and then the fountain, he was looking at the pier, but there was no raft. He rode right to the rocky shore and looked out across the water. The glassy lake did not reveal the path of the lost raft. He shook his head slowly then rode back up to basecamp as quick as he could and blasted through the door.

"It's gone! It's all gone," exclaimed Griffin.

"What are you talking about?" asked Maggie.

"The raft is gone, blown out across the lake, I guess," answered Griffin. "There is tree debris all over. It was quite a windstorm."

"Did you see the cable I added last night?" asked Cable.

"No, there was nothing left except a few broken cords that were still attached to the cleats on the pier."

The group, devastated, jogged to keep up with Griffin's pace. The ramifications were being processed by everyone—questions flooded their minds. Suddenly they were looking at the barren shore. They walked slowly to the pier and Mia reached down and touched the rough end of one of the severed dock lines.

Cable was scanning the scene and looking across the water for any sign of the raft when he said, "I came down here with the super long steel cable for our pump test and I attached it to the raft and the leg of the pier. Wait, is that it under the water?"

He pulled off his shoes and jumped into the water next to the piling.

He exclaimed, "The cable is still attached, but it slid down the post under the water. Where does it go?"

He reached down and pulled but it only stretched enough for him to get it out of the water, but it did not move.

"It goes sideways instead of out into the lake," Maggie noted from her position on the pier, "Can you follow it?"

"It goes too deep," said Cable. "Hand me that piece of cord."

He made a loop and put it around the cable so he could walk along the shore and still follow the cable that was pulled taut to the rocky bottom. Abby, Griffin, and Cable worked their way along the edge of the shore, not understanding where this was going. The others sat on the pier, with the heads in their hands or just looking out across the water.

"Do you think that the whole raft could have sunk?" asked Cable.

They worked further down the line until they were on the narrow sand between the plane wreck and the water where the beach arced back inland.

"The raft!" yelled Griffin. The group on the pier looked out across the lake and then at Griffin who was looking behind the plane. They jumped up and ran along the beach to catch up to the three who were walking to the raft. Sure enough, the wind came from the east during the night instead of the typical breeze from the north, so the raft was blown away from the pier.

"Cable, you saved us and..." Maggie trailed off. She hugged Cable and just stayed with her arms wrapped around him as she digested the loss, fear, and pain of their situation.

Uncomfortable with her sudden emotion or just uncomfortable with encountering his own fear and pain, Cable joked, "Well, I guess I earned my name yet again. Let's push this out so we can move it in the water. We should be able to pull it back with the cable from the end of the pier now."

Cody and Abby ran back to the pier and worked the cable gradually to the end as the tension eased. They kept pulling and the raft glided along the still water until it reached the pier.

"Now that we know that we get strong wind from the east let's tie it up on the windward side of the pier, so it blows into the pier instead of away," suggested Cable.

"I will see about making some steel cable dock lines," said Mia.

"For now, let's go eat breakfast and decompress for a bit and then we will get back to propulsion tests and checking all the lashings on the raft," proposed Maggie.

The group was exhausted, already at their emotional end and then experiencing devastating loss and then recovery all in one morning, all in one hour. They walked back to the pavilion and Sterling and Brent were eagerly waiting for news.

"We found it connected to the cable that Cable installed last night," said Abby. "It appears to be OK."

"Oh, I can't believe it," said Brent. "I have been thinking about all the possibilities, none of which were good. Do you want something to eat?"

"Ya, mostly just sit for a minute," said Cable.

Everyone sat, appearing numb and exhausted, nibbling on the typical breakfast menu.

After a while of silence, Abby said, "We need to get off this shore and get ourselves home. Let's start thinking bigger picture. We have been focused on the raft and propulsion, but we need to plan for all contingencies beyond the lake. How do we know where to land? Can we find binoculars to get a view before we leave? How much food will we take with us? What tools should we bring? What obstacles might we encounter after landing? We have to keep our head in the game and whoever is not testing the pump or fixing the raft needs to build a plan and lists. We also need two more planks removed from the dining tables. Griff, Cable, are you ready to test? Let's go."

Shelbi followed, "I will stay here with Brent and work on a plan. Who is going to the raft and who is staying here?"

"I am going to go with Cable to see if I can make new dock lines and then will meet at the shore," said Mia.

"I can head down there right now," said Cody.

"Do you think that I am more valuable here or at the raft?" asked Maggie.

"You are the careful planner," said Shelbi. "Stay with us and let's plan how to leave DreamLand."

Mia caught up to the propulsion crew on the driveway up to the shed.

"Cable, where did you find the steel cable, and did you find any fittings or any other hardware to make dock lines?" asked Mia.

"It was in the shed, hanging on the wall," replied Cable. "We can see if there is anything else. We only need a couple meters of material."

"I think we might as well move the generator and pump with all our fittings, hoses, ratchet straps, tools down to the shore. We might just leave the van down there for now so let's make sure we have all the heavy bits," said Griffin.

Cable helped Mia locate some other steel cable. They found two lengths that were heavier gauge and already had a loop end fitting on one end of each. They used a few links of chain to make another end fitting by looping the cable through the links and they were ready to go. Abby and Griffin had been loading the van and were ready to go when Mia had her new dock lines done.

They fired up the van and headed for the dining pavilion. Brent had just removed the second plank and Cable hopped out to put it in the back of the van and move a few branches that were blocking the west path down to the shore. They unloaded everything onto the pier and got to work laying the hoses onto the raft. After prototyping, moving, and agonizing over the mounting location and attachment, they chose to put the pump in the left-side log but keep the generator up on the plank. Cody and Mia had been checking and fixing minor details on the raft and then returned to basecamp to contribute to the big picture planning.

"I think we are ready to fire up the generator and run the pump," said Griffin. "Dip the inlet end into the water and let's point the nozzle away from the raft and the van, maybe aim for the plane. Here goes."

Griffin switched on the fuel and power, dialed the choke to full and pulled the cord. After the 4th or 5th pull, the generator coughed to life and putted along then he moved the choke to normal. He looked at Cable who was holding the inlet hose in the lake and then at Abby who was standing like a firefighter with the nozzle, who gave him a nod. He plugged the pump cord into the generator, which changed sound again and started the pump squealing briefly before there was a sputter of water from the nozzle and then an arc of water that nearly hit the plane. He turned it off.

"I think we have a propulsion system," said Griffin.

"There was quite a bit of force from the nozzle," said Abby. "I was surprised how much I had to lean into it. Let's transfer that leaning force to our raft."

"My end was less exciting," quipped Cable. "As a matter of fact, it kind of sucked."

"Oh, the puns are back," said Abby.

"I think we can just move this whole assembly," said Griffin. "I can carry the pump if each of you takes your end, yes, the sucky one and the one that blows."

"There we go, that's what I am talking about," said Cable. "Let's do it."

They picked up the water-spewing dragon and balanced their way across the planks and frames. Griffin lowered the pump into the log and guided the hoses out.

"How do the lengths look? We are still planning to cut these to fit," said Griffin.

"Mine is a little long but we can snip off a bit and put the elbow back on," said Cable.

"I am not sure how we want to hold or mount the nozzle. I can picture that we want to move it easily but not sure we want to try to hold it for the whole journey," said Abby. "We want it to go through the virtual center of this raft, like the c of g. If we aim too high or low, we cause the raft to tip fore and aft. Steering should be a matter of pivoting to give us a thrust vector around our pivot point. With these 2 rows of logs, I don't think we need a keel since we are more like a catamaran."

"It sounds like you just designed it," said Cable. "Once we dial in the elevation angle, we want to be able to pivot it side to side. That feels like a tripod contraption to me."

"But it sounds like more weight to me," said Griffin. "There are 9 tripods that are already on this cruise."

"True, true," said Cable. "Like Mr. Alpin would say, 'If it ain't broke, it doesn't have enough features yet.' Engineers are always tempted to engineer a solution when the best solution might be to stop. What's the problem we need to solve? If we are worried about fatigue, maybe all we need is a way to rest the nozzle in something that reacts the force. Maybe just the back of the van. No, we don't want the forces to go through our wheel straps or push the van off the raft. It would have to attach to the raft frame. Could it just be some baling wire that holds the nozzle to this bed frame and then someone just directs the flow?"

"Now, that's a solution," confirmed Griffin. "How does our hose length look?"

"If we mount it here, we need to cut about 20 cm," said Abby.

"Go ahead while I rig a way to run the extension cord under the frames but keep them out of the water," said Griffin.

"Good idea," quipped Cable. "I will run up to get that baling wire."

While Cable was gone, Griffin looped the extension cord under the frames so it would not get run over or tripped over. Abby cut the hose and positioned the nozzle so that it would pivot on the rear frame and most of the force would be reacted directly through the raft and all the pilot had to do is hold the position. Cable returned just when Abby was ready to mount it. Griffin cut off a bunch of 10 cm pieces of wire to make tie wraps and went to work. Cable took one piece to the front to position the inlet hose in the water.

"I think that if I wrap a figure-8 of wire around the narrow throat of the nozzle and the frame, we will get what we want," said Abby as she started wrapping the spool, over, around, crossing, under, around, crossing, and back up the other side, repeating a dozen times. She pulled back on the nozzle to simulate the thrust force and then maneuvered it.

"It's pretty good, but I think we need it tighter. Can you hand me that screwdriver, Cable?" asked Abby.

This caught the attention of both boys and they stopped to watch as Abby wrapped more wire around the neck of the first wire loops and also around the shaft of the screwdriver. She cut the wire off and then twisted the screwdriver like a handle and the wire loops constricted around the neck. She kept trying the nozzle movement and adjusted the tension with the screwdriver. When she was done, she looked up to see both boys with their eyes and mouth in mid-trance.

"What? Never seen that before?" asked Abby playfully. "You can generate enormous forces by twisting wire or rope."

"That's the most beautiful thing I have seen in a while," joked Griffin. "Let's fire this up. Release the short dock lines but keep the long one attached for the test."

Cable grabbed the paddles and laid them on the planks. Abby was stationed at the nozzle, Griffin at the generator. The raft gently bobbed in the water and the typical breeze flowed down from their DreamLand mountain. Griffin checked his connections and settings and pulled the starter cord. It started and as soon as it ran smooth, he looked at Abby and plugged it in. The generator noise increased, and water started spurting from the nozzle. Within a few seconds, the steady stream was flowing, and the raft started sliding past the pier. As it entered the open water, the raft was rotating slightly so Abby slid the nozzle a few centimeters along the frame and tried some angle adjustments until the raft was moving straight. When the placement was right, Abby twisted the screwdriver a bit more to lock the location. About the time that it was moving as she hoped, the cable went taut and she had to attempt a U-turn. Since the thrust vector was out the stern and so was the taut cable, no amount of angle would do much, so she signaled to Griffin to cut the power. At that moment, the screwdriver slipped from her hands and disappeared into the cold, dark lake.

Abby noted, "That worked well, but I forgot that I can't do a U-turn. I can only do sweeping turns. This is a good lesson learned that we cannot back up if we get into trouble. We need to see trouble ahead to make course corrections. And screwdrivers don't float, just in case you were wondering."

"We could add reverse," Cable joked. "Actually, if you spin that nozzle and point it under the van you should be able to reverse. For now, I will just spin us with a paddle. Let's try going back to the pier and try steering."

The team did several more runs until they were comfortable with the operation and limitations of the system.

"I feel good about this," said Abby. "Let's conserve our fuel. Hmm, thinking about fuel, how much should we bring?"

Griffin paused. "Good point. We don't know where we are going or how far anything is or how efficient our water jet is or how far it is across the lake or much of anything, now that I think about it. Water is about 9 pounds per gallon and most fuels are less, like 7 pounds per gallon. Those barrels are 50 gallons, so it would be another 350 pounds or 150 kilos. *Oooff.* That is another .15 cubic meters of displacement. It is what it is. It would be silly to get to the other side and not be able to drive out to civilization or worse that we don't get to the other side. OK, we need to find a place for 40-50 gallons of fuel, maybe split it into 2 of those blue 20-gallon drums and put one on each side in the logs."

"Since kerosene is lighter than water, we could float the barrel, but it would cause a lot of drag. Never mind," said Cable as he countered his own idea.

"Let's tie up," said Abby. "I think we have enough testing to know how it will work. We will be adding a bunch of weight, but the physics is about the same. More weight will be more displacement and slower speed, but our direction control will be similar with the two pontoons. Let's launch our prototype. We can leave the pump connected, but take the generator into the van and leave the van down here, right?"

"I agree," said Griffin.

The three of them hustled around putting away the generator, ramps, and paddles, using the new steel dock lines. They stood on the pier, together, looking out across the water, at the plane, at the raft, and back across the water.

"We can do this," whispered Cable. Silently, they walked back up the familiar path to DreamLand. They could hear the conversation as they approached, not heated, but quite energetic.

"How's it going?" asked Cable.

"Great," said Maggie as she greeted Cable with a hug. "Look at our plans. We have discussed food, water, shelter, packing, 10 essentials, and some contingency plans."

"How about fuel?" asked Griffin. "We were just noodling about that one on the pier."

"Speaking of the pier, how did the testing go?" asked Brent.

"Great!" said Abby. "We went back and forth several times and adjusted the nozzle and tried steering. But we are worried about fuel and how much is the right amount. Show us your plans."

Shelbi stood up and rested her knee on a bench for balance instead of using her crutch. "First, we had to establish a timeline. We allocated 1 day for the traverse of the lake. If this is an amusement park it must be within 1 to 1.5 hours of some city center when traveling at highway speed. We figure there is a large parking lot on the other side of the lake, and they ran ferries across to both sides of the pier for arrivals and departures. Anyway, timeline. 1 hour of driving could be as far as 60 miles or 100 km, too far for us to walk without backpacks and supplies, so we did conclude we want to take the van. We figure there could be obstacles like the downed trees and gates that we have found here in the park. Even with those issues, we figure that it should not take more than 3 days of driving. Theoretically, we could live with no food for that long, but we are thinking to just bring rice and leave the heavy food cans here. We would need some kerosene to boil our water, but now I am getting into the food discussion."

Maggie continued, "We think we can get away with 1 drum of water. 9 people x 3 days x 1 gallon each is 27 gallons and those blue drums are about 20 gallons and we can fill a couple of the water bottles from the plane for each person. For tools we are planning on a long prybar, saw, screwdrivers, basically any tool that we have used so far. Also, since we will have the generator, Brent suggested Mr. Alpin's favorite tool, the angle grinder for any chains or gates. For clothing, we have figured out our bare minimum, a few layers and our waterproof jackets. Since we are coming into summer, the days have been getting warmer, not colder, but we might get rain. We will bring the matches from the kitchen so we will have a source of fire for each day. We were just talking about shelter when you arrived. Nine of us cannot sleep in the van so we need some shelter and Mia was telling us about the rubberized canvas flag that we could all sleep under to keep warm. We were joking about it really being DreamLand."

They chuckled.

"I like your assumptions about distance and timing and your lists. What happens if we find a landslide across the road?" asked Griffin. "What's our contingency for water and shelter?"

A cloud moved overhead, and the room darkened, as if on cue.

"We figure we can't possibly have that bad of luck, right?" joked Sterling as she got up and went into the kitchen.

"It doesn't have to be a pretty solution, but we need to think if we would do anything differently if everything goes sideways," said Griffin.

"What could possibly go—" started Cable.

"Don't jinx it," blurted Mia and Cable laughed.

"Are we ready to do this tomorrow?" asked Griffin.

"Tomorrow? So soon?" asked Maggie. "I thought we would have more time, but I guess is there anything else we really need to do besides pack up?"

"That's why I am asking," said Griffin. "We have our raft, pump, generator, paddles all ready."

"I think packing will take longer than we think, and we don't want to start too late that we will still be on the water after dark," said Maggie.

"Ever the practical one," said Cable. "We do have to fill water and fuel drums so maybe we get an early start and see what it looks like."

"Dinner is ready," said Sterling. "By the way, thank you all for including me in today's discussions."

The group gathered around the table to eat.

"Could we pray?" asked Cody. People nodded and shrugged and tipped their heads down. "Heavenly Father, we thank you for your protection and wisdom in these times. We thank you for each person in this room and the skills you have woven together in this group. We thank you for Sterling and her service and kindness. We pray that you would guide and protect us in our journey forward. Amen." And the group repeated, "Amen." Sterling put her arm around Cody.

Sterling softly said to Cody. "I was going down a really bad road and you all have saved me. I have not been a nice person in my past, but you have taken care of me. Thank you."

Uncomfortable with emotion, Cody joked, "Well, this road isn't over yet. But we should make it."

Cable served himself two rice patties and stepped outside. "Hey guys, it's really pretty out here, warm too."

The clouds had drifted over and were streaked with color with reds in the east, pinks above and orange and yellow in the west over the lake and the plane wreckage. From the edge of the dining pavilion if one looked through the overgrown trees one could just barely see parts of the beach and plane from their elevated perspective. The group filed outside one by one, Sterling carrying Brent's plate and Mia helping Shelbi. They sat and ate, watching the changing colors fade to gray with only a blush of color in the west.

As everyone moved back inside it was much darker, so everyone laid down except Griffin. He was bumping around in the kitchen storeroom looking at blue drums. Cable joined him and clicked on his phone light.

Griffin explained, "I am seeing that we have 4 of these, 2 we can use for fuel and 1 for water. I was smelling them to see what was in them. I don't smell much except the plastic smell that comes from closed containers. This one appears to be the cleanest, so I was going to fill it with water. Wanna help?"

"Sure," said Cable.

"The others we will fill with kerosene at the warehouse in the morning," said Griffin. "I think we can just put this on the dolly and ride it down the hill. 20 gallons times 8.4 plus the container is about 180 pounds, like me. No problem."

"Maybe in the morning light, right?" said Cable. "Let's roll this outside so we aren't banging around in the morning."

After maneuvering it outside, they paused and looked out across the lake, the sky was quite dark now with the ceiling of clouds.

"What is that?" asked Cable. "Look, there."

"What am I looking at?" asked Griffin.

"Do you see the glow in the clouds? We haven't had this type of cloud ceiling before, so we haven't seen it. It appears to be coming from behind the largest ridge across the lake. I still don't see any direct light, but there is definitely a glow."

"You are right," said Griffin. "I am not sure what that tells us except confirming that our assumption about a city being over the hills. We have to assume that there is only one road that leaves the dock and takes us to the city, just based on logic. If there were a highway, we would be seeing headlights. It does indicate that we should turn east and then go south, if there is any choice, to go toward the glow."

"Maybe this is what Cody was praying for when he asked for guidance. A glow in the sky, kind of like the Christmas story," said Cable. "Let's go to bed."

CHAPTER 25 — LAUNCH

*There is only one thing stronger than all the armies of the world:
and that is an idea whose time has come.   - Victor Hugo*

The morning came early since sleep was less restful with the heavy expectations of the next couple of days. Cable and Griffin were up just as the sky started to glow, and the rest of the group rose as they heard whooping and hollering fade away down the hill.

"What was that? Is everything OK?" asked Mia.

"Ya, just those boys riding their water drum down the hill," said Abby dryly with a twinkle of a smile as she came back in from the front pavilion.

"They rode the water drum?" asked Brent.

"Well, it was on two dollies and they rode it like a pony through the brush," said Abby.

The group was busy eating, packing and checking things. Mia, Abby, and Cody took the other two blue drums to the tool shed to pull out any tools that would be useful and put them in a bucket.

"I figure the bucket is another tool," said Abby. "We can use it to carry water or anything else."

"Good plan," said Cody.

Cable and Griffin walked in as they were carrying the bucket outside.

"We got the water moved and now we are going to fill the drums that I see you brought over. Thank you," said Griffin.

"What do you think about the tin snips?" asked Cody.

"We used them for many things, and they are small so we probably should," said Cable as he put them in the bucket.

"Did you guys eat already?" asked Abby.

"Yep, we are good," said Cable. "We are going to fill these up and take them down to the raft and drive the van up to meet you in DreamLand. By the way, Cody, your prayers worked last night. When we rolled the water drum outside after dark, Griff and I could see the glow of a city coming over the east end of that ridge across the lake. No direct lights, but at least it guided the way."

"What? That's awesome," said Cody.

He and Griffin carried the blue drums into the warehouse. Abby and Cody carried the bucket and other supplies down to the raft and Mia headed back to basecamp to share the plan and update the group.

As she joined the group in the main room, Mia reported, "Griff and Cable are filling the blue drums with fuel and Abby and Cody are taking the tools to the raft and we will all meet up here as soon as everything is done. The weather is nice, and the water looked smooth from the ring road with only a tiny breeze. Oh, and on another note, Cable and Griff saw a glow of a distant city over the ridge across the lake last night."

"Are you kidding me?" asked Shelbi. "What? Civilization? Are we done packing? I am ready to go home."

"Are we doing this today?" asked Mia.

"Like you said, the weather is good, and we are packed up an hour after sunrise, whatever time that is," said Shelbi.

Mia realized that the group had stopped thinking about time as a number and more about where the sun is in the sky. In a way, it was freeing, no longer defined by numbers on some schedule that hangs on the prison wall to tell the inmates when to eat, have yard time, and sleep. Her life was orchestrated down to the minute - school, golf practice, Chinese school, homework, cello practice, and sleep, and the punishment is severe if any of those plans deviate. The strict schedule is still better than the year she had to live with her uncle before her parents moved from China to join her. Those are scars that she kept hidden from everyone, even her mom, especially her mom.

"Mia. Mia," called Shelbi. "Where did you go? We have been calling you."

"Right here. I was right here," whispered Mia.

"Are you ready? Let's go home," said Shelbi.

"Yep," Mia said as she turned and dabbed a tear with her sleeve. "In some ways, I will miss this place and this time with you. I felt safer here with you than I have in other times of my life."

The group carried their stuff to the pavilion and shortly thereafter the van came lurching along the weedy path. They opened the back doors and loaded their small bags, blankets, rice, cookpot, a few other essentials, and Brent, Shelbi, and Sterling. The van continued along the path for the longer route down the hill while the group walked quickly down the shorter route. By the time they had arrived, they had unloaded the passengers on the pier and were lining up the van with the ramps.

The water was still glassy, and the breeze was slight. The sun was only an hour above the eastern ridge. Looks like a good day for a cruise. Griffin was in the van, idling, while Abby and Cody were doing final adjustments with the ramps. Cable was connecting fuel and power lines.

Abby stood up on the raft and motioned Griffin to coast forward. Cody and Cable were stabilizing the raft with the levers while everyone else was on the pier. Abby gave a double hand signal to move forward, but slowly, and Griffin eased out the clutch and the van moved along the ramps. This time Abby warned Griffin about the approaching drop to the planks and motioned to turn a finger-width to the left while she backed her way down the plank. One more drop as the rear tires found their home on the planks. About half a meter later, Abby crossed her arms and Griffin clutched, set the brake, and shut off the engine. Everyone released their captive breath.

Cable had already laid out the ratcheting straps, so everyone got to work feeding the strap through the wheels and down past the planks and the handrails and back up to the wheel. *Clickity, click*, the van was getting cinched down until the tires bulged at the bottom. Meanwhile, Griffin and Cody had loaded the generator and were lashing it to the center of raft next to the van where the extension cord was already hanging.

Cable checked the position of the water inlet hose and fitting and then the outlet nozzle that was about 60 cm from the back of the van, enough room for the pilot to sit and direct the flow. Cable placed one paddle along each side of the van and then checked the status of the interior of the van. Items were stowed near the center, but he reached in and grabbed the spool of cord and hung it from the tow hitch, just in case it was needed.

Griffin said, "Let's have Brent and Shelbi sit inside the forward logs and the rest of us can stand on the planks or in the logs as we are able and see how we are balanced. Also, we found 4 life vests. They should be worn by our 4 weakest swimmers."

Everyone moved into position as the raft bobbed a bit with the shifting of weight. Brent, Sterling, Shelbi, and Mia put on the vests. Griffin ran along the pier checking the balance. He called, "Do all the logs look dry inside?"

"All dry up front," said Brent.

"All dry in the rear," said Cody.

"Firing up the generator, but no pump yet," yelled Griffin as he turned on the switch and choke. With one last pause and glance to the front and then the rear, he saw Abby with a smile and thumbs up. He pulled the cord once, twice, sputter, and a third time, *poppity-pop, purrrrr.*

"Pull the dock lines!" Griffin yelled.

"Go for launch!" called Cable.

Abby steadied the nozzle and Griffin plugged the extension cord to the generator. With a spurt and a blast, there was a column of water coming from the rear. Just as the Saturn V seems to pause too long while the fiery cloud billows out on the launch pad, the raft did not move at first, but then the pier started to drift by.

"We are moving!" yelled Shelbi. "It's working!"

The raft cleared the pier as the column of water continued to stream from the stern.

"Remember, we need eyes looking out front for any signs of a pier or road or anything," called Griffin over the rattle and hum of the generator. "Also, check for leaks, loose straps, or anything else that looks wrong. It's not a pleasure cruise. If something goes wrong, get out of the logs so you don't get pulled under."

Everyone looked at each other awkwardly and then at the distant shoreline. Abby was aiming the raft for the middle of the opposite shore, seeing as that would be the shortest route, until they determined otherwise. The shape of the lake was becoming more apparent as they moved away from their DreamLand. It was longer than it was wide, and the DreamLand park was located along the only level shoreline that they could see, with steep, rocky cliffs into the lake on either side.

More quietly, Griffin said to Cable, "That is the kind of coastline I am afraid of on the other side. We have to find that pier or landing."

After a while of listening to the droning sound of the generator, the pier that they had left was almost invisible. The lake surface had lost its glossy sheen and was textured and dark.

"I see something white and geometric," said Maggie. "Pretty much dead ahead."

Everyone leaned forward as if it would make the shore closer.

"I think I see what you are talking about," said Shelbi.

"Me too," said Griffin. "Looks like tall poles, right?"

"Do you see something, Griff?" asked Abby, since she could only see the departing shore from her position at the nozzle.

"I think so," replied Griffin. "Aim a bit more to the right, but not much. Everyone, keep your eyes open for other things in case that is not the pier."

"I think I am seeing more structure to the left of the poles," said Brent.

"I see it too," said Maggie.

"Steady as you go, Abby," said Griffin.

"OK," replied Abby. "That's good because I can hardly see our shore except for the Ferris wheel."

Sterling had been silent for the entire voyage, entranced by the precision of the execution of the plan, gripping the edges of the log with her creamy, white hands.

"There is a pier, on the left end!" yelled Mia.

"Copy," called Griffin. "Abby, we will need to go a bit to the left so let's bank now to reduce the correction angle."

The lake was more choppy than when they started and the raft dipped and rolled with each wave. Abby rotated the nozzle and the raft began to turn.

"OK, hold there," said Griffin.

Suddenly there was a loud pop and water was spraying everywhere while the rear hose bounced around and then there was a splash. Abby had been perched on the frame between the van and the edge of the water but when the hose let loose it knocked Abby over the edge. Griffin pulled the extension cord and shut down the generator. Cable slid a paddle out to the rear. Abby's strength powered her through the water just as Cable dropped the paddle in front of her and she grabbed the metal sign. The sudden drag slowed the raft and they pulled Abby onto the plank between Griffin and Cable.

"That was cold and unexpected," said Abby. "What happened?"

She looked over at the nozzle and the hose. "We never glued the last joint after we trimmed the hose the final time."

Abby reached up to move her wet hair from her face and there was blood on her face and running down her arm and dripping off her elbow.

"Hold on, we have a situation," said Cable. "What hurts? Where did you get cut?"

"Cut? Nothing hurts," said Abby.

"Your hand. It's coming from your right hand," said Griffin.

She lifted her hand and a long gash was leaking blood onto her wet arm. Griffin pulled off his shirt and wrapped it around her hand.

"We all know you have the great water polo bod. You don't have to show off," joked Abby. "I think I cut it on the paddle. I'm glad I have the adrenaline right now, but we should probably get a move on."

The others had been trying to see what was going on and whispering updates. Cable spoke up, "So, we had an anomaly here in the stern. Abby went for a swim and cut her hand, but we have it wrapped up. The high-pressure side of the propulsion system has blown off and we might be able to repair it. The elbow fitting is gone too. It might take more work to repair. Any ideas would be welcome."

"Is Abby OK?" asked Shelbi.

"Ya, I'm fine," said Abby.

"Um, there is a nice breeze," said Mia.

"Thanks for the weather report and the positive vibe," said Abby.

"No, I have been thinking about the breeze and wondering if we could sail this raft. Do we have that DreamLand sign?"

"Yes, I think so," said Cable. "I think I saw it in the van. Hold on."

Cable stood up and balanced on the frame and opened the rear door. He crawled inside and the group could hear banging and sliding.

"A-ha! Yes. What do you have in mind?" asked Cable.

"How about we use your two paddles and lash that sign up as a big sail like we did on the Colorado River trip?"

"I like it," said Cable as he exited the van and closed the rear door. "Cody, flip that paddle over so the sharp end is up and let's tie the sign to the paddle. Actually, let's tie the bottom corners to the raft first and then the tops."

They unfolded the flag, which was about twice the width as the raft, and tied the bottom corners to the furthest corners of the logs. With some tricky balancing, Cable and Cody were able to attach the top corner to Cody's paddle and then the other to Cable's.

"Ready, let's lift," said Cable as the two poles were pushed up and the sail tightened immediately.

"That's working," said Griffin. The raft was starting to move past bubbles in the water as the flag was taut. "How is our trajectory?"

Shelbi and Brent looked to the shore and to each other and back to the shore. Brent said, "It looks about right for now, but we might need to aim left. It's working. Great idea Mia!"

The raft was a bit slower, or seemed slower, without the sound of the generator and water spraying, but they were moving toward the shore.

Griffin asked, "Is there any way that we can prop that pole up or give me the pole so you can move to the back and see if you can work on the propulsion in case we need some vector adjustment?"

Cable handed the pole to Griffin and moved toward Cody to retrieve the hose. He moved it around and tried bending it to make up for the missing elbow fitting.

"Well, we can create thrust, but it will not be at the center so it may cause us to turn," said Cable. "If I can get more slack, I could bend it and get it closer to the center. Try moving the pump back and sliding the inlet hose back."

Everyone on the pump side of the raft started lifting and sliding components while Cody and Griffin kept the sail taut. Progress is difficult to measure when there is nothing to compare to, but it seemed like objects were getting clearer even if they did not seem closer yet. Eventually, the pump was moved about half a meter to the rear and the inlet hose had to be detached and moved to the inboard side of the log pontoon. By now they could make out a pier, the white lamp posts for the parking lot, and some smaller buildings.

Brent observed, "Our trajectory is not bad, but we are heading for the parking lot that appears to have a seawall and not a shore. I can't tell how tall it is so it would be better if we moved to the left to intercept the pier or the shoreline to the left of the pier."

"We could try the pump or just change our relative drag," said Maggie.

"What do you mean?" asked Griffin.

"It means that someone on the left side of the boat could put their foot in the water and the raft should turn left," answered Maggie.

"Let's try the pump and maybe we will move faster too," said Griffin. "Cable, are you ready for thrust?"

Cable braced himself and created a curve in the hose to aim out the stern with no nozzle, "Fire away."

Griffin adjusted the choke and pulled on the cord. Nothing, not even a sputter. Again, and again he pulled but nothing. The shore was definitely getting closer and the seawall was looking taller than their raft. No one had noticed that the ripple on the lake had turned to small waves with the increasing wind and the van was rocking on the small raft. Overturning now would be catastrophic and so would smashing into the seawall. They were now aware of their closing velocity as they approached the seawall. Maggie stuck her feet in the water and the raft slowly turned. When it looked like the raft trajectory and wind direction were going to combine for the right vector to the pier, she pulled her feet back into the log.

"That works too," said Griffin. "Isn't physics great."

The raft was coming ashore between the pier and the seawall, a space large enough for the bigger ferry boats of the past and perfect for their tiny landing craft. The forward logs ran aground on the rocky bottom and Griffin hopped out with the small waves lapping at his feet. He pushed the raft out a bit and floated it to the pier, a few meters to the left. Cable jumped out and wrapped a dock line to the cleat and the group cheered.

"We did it!" exclaimed Shelbi.

"Um, we forgot our ramps," said Cable. "I intended to slide them under the van but forgot with everything going on. Do you think we can drive off?"

"The planks are more than half a meter off the ground," said Brent. "What if we drive forward onto the front planks and then move the rear ones up and use them as ramps?"

"That's it. I meant to do that. To save weight and all," joked Cable.

"Riiiight. We better do it quick because the waves are intensified at the shore and we are really starting to rock," rallied Griffin.

Everyone started untying cords and loosening straps and Griffin hopped in the van. Sterling helped Abby, the newest casualty, to the pier and the others made their way up to the shore. Cable guided Griffin to move forward to clear the rear planks. Cody and Maggie slid them forward and Cable made last adjustments to get them lined up. The raft was rising and falling, so the boards were a bit of a moving target. Popping the clutch more briskly than intended, the van tires squealed on the wet planks and jumped forward. The front tires reached the ground just as the ramps dropped off the raft and the van bounced and skidded up the rocky shore.

"You were right about these vans crossing rivers and now they have even crossed lakes," joked Cable as the group exhaled a nervous chuckle.

"If everyone is ok, I am going to pull the van up to those benches so we can work out our next plan," said Griffin.

"Before you do, let's put the fuel drums in the van," suggested Maggie.

"Good point," said Griffin. "Maggie, did your planning determine if we take or leave the generator?"

"We couldn't think of any big reason to take it except to run the angle grinder and right now the generator isn't running."

Griffin suggested, "Let's put it ashore in case we need to come back for it. Wait. Tie the heavy dock lines to the tow hitch. I have an idea."

Maggie moved the side dock lines to the front and then dropped the loop on the hitch ball and moved out of the way. Griffin eased out the clutch and started dragging the raft out of the water. Once the weight distribution moved from the water to the rocks, the raft and van could not move until a small wave lifted the raft and it made one last hop and Griffin shut off the engine.

"Let's offload that water, fuel, and generator and tie this off to the pier now," said Griffin. "At least the raft should stay here in case we need it again."

"Need it again?" asked Shelbi. "I sure hope we don't need this again. I don't think my heart could take another trip like that."

The crew slid the water and fuel drums and generator into the back of the van and Brent and Shelbi sat in the open doors at the back. Abby waved off an offer to sit in the front seat "My hand is cut, not my feet," she said bluntly.

Griffin moved the van to the level ground in front of a low building that looked like it might house the restrooms and ticket sales. Faded signs pointed to brighter times at DreamLand.

"Look at the prices," said Maggie.

"What? Are you impressed with the great deal we had?" joked Cable.

"No, they are in Czech koruna, not Euros, so we are in the Czech Republic, not Germany," observed Maggie.

"Great, we aren't lost," said Brent dryly.

Shelbi unwrapped Abby's hand and flushed it with some water. She pulled out some ointment and gauze from the first aid kit and handed Griffin's shirt back to him with a big blood stain in the center of the chest.

Griffin put it on and joked, "Looks like we've been in battle."

"We have," stated Sterling.

Griffin asked, "So, what do we think about the generator? I think we leave it here and we will come back if we need it, so it will give us enough room in the van. The only thing we have that needs power is the angle grinder since our phones are charged and turned off, right?"

"Sounds good to me," said Maggie.

"Me too," said Brent. "Has anyone tried their phone over here?"

"I did, but got nothing," said Shelbi.

"I have strapped the drums to the sides of the van for us to sit on," said Cable. "I think Brent ought to sit in the front seat with his knee and if we pile some luggage up there someone can sit on the doghouse."

Shelbi said, "I am fine wherever. By the way, everyone should be drinking their water. Keep hydrated. How long until we leave? I need to find a bush."

"Or use the bathroom," offered Griffin. The glass in the door is broken. I'm headed over to see if we can get in."

"I'm coming too," said Maggie.

Griffin loped over and reached his arm through the glass and opened the door. A few minutes later, he returned to the entrance. "Bathroom anyone? 3rd hallway down, the 1st door for bathrooms. No water, but there are seats and privacy. We will leave as soon as everyone is ready."

Everyone filed in as Griffin returned to the van to check the load. Cable returned first and they stood, leaning against the hood.

"Well, we made it this far," said Cable. "Are we ready for the next challenge?"

CHAPTER 26 — THE DRIVE

You can do anything as long as you have the passion, the drive, the focus, and the support. - Sabrina Bryan

Everyone loaded into the van and found their spot, Griffin, Shelbi, and Brent up front, the other 6 down in 2 rows in the back. Everyone focused on the view forward.

Griffin connected the wires, yellow, red, and then orange and the van awoke again. It was still before midday. Although Cody and Shelbi both checked for signal, no one bothered to check their phones for the time anymore. Time, as a number, still belonged in the other world.

The van bumped forward and climbed the road out of the parking lot. Grass was growing from every crack and the brush had left about one lane down the middle of the road. Griffin did well avoiding branches, rocks, and other debris.

"Your racing experience was good training for this road," said Brent. "Have you noticed that the grass in the cracks is the same height across the whole road? Wouldn't that mean this road has not been getting any traffic, not limited traffic, none?"

"Oh well. Doesn't change our plan."

"Hey, check our odometer. 100 km or bust, right?" said Shelbi.

"That's what we think," said Maggie.

"31,419 km," said Griffin.

The road was a bit like life, without a painted line down the center, but rather had a series of faded dots that provided guidance, except for the occasional obstacle that required Griffin to swerve. It was eerie to travel a road that must have seen thousands of happy families on their way to adventure and fun, but now it whimpered with rejection and decay.

"Whoa! Hold on!" called Griffin as he braked sharply and swerved to a stop between a large boulder and the edge of the road.

"Can we squeeze by," asked Maggie.

"I don't think we can move a rock that is a meter tall so that's all we can do, unless we want to walk 95 km, or however much further we have," said Griffin. "I need to approach this boulder from this angle near the edge of the road and they don't believe in guardrails. I will need to get up on this berm and then come around the boulder but turn tight to get around these rocks and do it with a clutch and stick. I need a couple spotters. And prayers are welcome, too, Cody."

Griffin backed up the van and then bumped and jerked up onto the berm until Cody gave direction to turn sharply left. The van responded begrudgingly but got hung up on the boulder just in front of the rear wheel. The group lunged at the van and pushed it away and it scraped the last meter then turned right. Doing so caused the bumper to catch and bend out at a crazy angle, but the van made it through.

Everyone piled back in and Griffin went back to the slow task of slaloming through the detritus of an aging attraction in a natural world. The next 10 minutes was less eventful.

The forest trees loomed high into the sky at the sides of the road. Their proximity guaranteed that their cast-off branches would land on the road, but most were small and allowed the van to trample them at slow speeds. As the road was hidden behind a small rise, the van was greeted with a tree that was laying across the road, from within the trees on the right and wedged between trees on the left.

"That's unfortunate," said Griffin as he slowed and stopped with his bumper nearly touching the tree, as if he were approaching a parking lot red and white striped arm that should be opening at any moment. This was not moving on its own. Most of the crew hopped out and surveyed the scene.

"What's the problem we need to solve?" asked Mia.

"Pretty obvious that we have a tree we need to move, right?" said Brent.

"No, the problem is we need to get by the tree. Over. Under. Through. Or Around," stated Shelbi.

Griffin placed his foot against it and pushed to characterize its strength, stiffness, and weight. "Most of the branches snapped off when it hit the ground, so it is probably old and might snap if we push on it," he said. "I am going to put the bumper up to the tree and give it a push. Someone spot me, stand clear in case something breaks."

Griffin moved the van forward until the bumper pressed against the middle of the trunk and then gave it fuel. The tree moved and bowed a bit but did not snap. He clutched it and rolled back a ways and then popped the clutch and hit the throttle and it crashed into the trunk and, as it did, the bumper rode up on the trunk.

Cable said, "Back up a meter. I have an idea."

Cable started throwing branches and logs into the road from the surrounding area and others did the same. He stacked the largest limbs up against the trunk and then stacked the smaller ones in front and above the larger ones before it. He moved and adjusted the limbs as he compared the location to the wheelbase of the van.

"Griff, drive straight ahead and keep your momentum as we get behind you to push." The group gathered behind the van, except for Brent and Shelbi who had gotten out to make the van lighter but were sitting on another nearby log. Griffin punched it and the van started bouncing up the stack of logs and the group came to push on the back doors. There was scraping and skidding. As the front wheels started down the back side, the van was sliding across the log on its belly but its driving tires in the rear were not able to reach the ground. The group pushed as the van rocked forward, and the rear tires started skidding on the logs. They rocked it and the van launched over the last hurdle. The group sat down on the log. Griffin shut off the van and sat down with everyone else.

"Thanks," he said. "That has to be the last of the challenges, right?"

"Don't jinx it," said Mia.

"Shelbi said, "Let's have some water and see if we can get out now. It is midafternoon and we have a few hours of light left."

"This would explain the lack of traffic beyond this point," said Griffin.

"Let's go," said Brent.

They all loaded back up in the van and continued winding through the mountainous road and avoiding obstacles. Nobody said anything, but they probably noticed that there were just as many branches and weeds as before. Each time they came around a curve they all looked expectantly as far as they could see. On their right was a river that was flowing and tumbling along through the rocks and on the left was the steep mountainside that was covered in trees.

The canyon kept bending and the river seemed to squeeze the road with only room for a few reflective white pickets to mark the edge. As they swerved to avoid a few rocks that had tumbled down and rounded a curve they were not sure what they were seeing, or rather not seeing.

At first, they tried to comprehend what they were looking at. In front of them was the same mountain slope and the same river, but there was no road in between. The mountain seemed to have melted and swallowed the flat surface and the river gnawed at the pavement until there was nothing to share between them. The van came to rest at the edge of this new mountain and Griffin just put his head on the steering wheel as they sat in silence.

"That's a problem," said Cable, devoid of his normal humor. He got out of the van and swung the door almost shut, the cool breeze was blowing down the canyon. Griffin joined him as they stood and looked at the next impossible situation. "This explains the road and maybe the park closure. I wonder if this happened and it was too expensive to repair to keep the park open."

"I can't even tell if there is enough pavement underneath if we tried to dig," said Cable.

"And there are too many rocks and slope to try to tackle this now," added Griffin.

The van door closed but no one turned to see who got out.

"What does it look like," asked Abby.

"It looks like we will not have Czech pizza tonight," said Cable, trying to lighten the moment.

Griffin observed, "It looks like half the road has disappeared into the river and the other half is filled with a mountain. It is too sloped to drive on. I'm so tired. Let's set up camp for the night and evaluate our situation. There are trees and rocks back there and perhaps some shelter from the wind."

Griffin got back into the van without saying anything and turned the van around to a sheltered spot in the trees a couple hundred meters from the slide. Cable turned on his phone and held it high, shook his head, and turned it off. The group gradually exited the van and got out the stove and food supplies. Sterling and Shelbi set up a kitchen on a large flat rock next to the van. Dinner was as simple and bland as the conversation, white rice.

The group ate in silence until Brent spoke, "This river probably flows out of the lake we crossed, but we did not see the outlet. I assume it was out of the eastern end of the lake. We could look at going back, leave the van, and riding the raft down the river past the slide. Eventually, it should flow to a town, right?"

"Or another lake and then we would be stuck with no van or food," said Shelbi.

"True. I was focused on getting around the slide."

"Let's think about that," started Maggie. "How far have we come since the lake?"

"I didn't look," said Griffin. "The odometer is not electronic so you can check."

Maggie opened the van door and looked at the gauge. "31,482, so we have gone about 66 km."

"Can we walk the rest of the way?" asked Sterling.

"Only if we split the group," said Brent. "At this point, we should be close enough that we should do it. I would just slow you down and would be fine to stay here at the van."

"So, should we leave most of the group and only send a couple runners for help or walk most of the group out and come back for a couple of us?" asked Shelbi.

"Let's look at the facts and figure out the problem we need to solve," said Cable. "We cannot get the van past this slide, so the only way out that I see is to walk. Not everyone can walk, so we are dividing the group. If we are dividing, it makes the most sense to risk as few people as possible who are the fastest. The minimum group would be 2-4. Who would that be?"

"Griff does water polo and I do soccer," said Maggie.

"I run and think we ought to have 3 in the runner group," said Cable. "That leaves Mia and Cody who are not injured back here."

"I just have a cut hand," said Abby. "But I get your point. We would still have a solid group here. If we think about the timing, the runners should be able to cover up to 30 km by nightfall if they leave first thing in the morning, so the most we would have to stay is one more night."

"What if they don't get to a town before dark?" asked Mia.

Cable observed, "Good point. It is probably too cold to spend the night without shelter, so we need to carry enough layers in case we need to hunker down."

Maggie stood up and said, "We will make some extra rice in the morning that we will carry with us, take our jackets and run first thing in the morning. With the nearly full moon, we can run on the pavement through the night. We will not stop until we find help."

"Leader Maggie has spoken, and we will make it so," said Cable.

Maggie chuckled, realizing she was the only one standing, and sat back down. The sky was changing colors with only a wisp of clouds that were streaked with pink. They pulled out their DreamLand flag and every layer they brought with them.

"Let's set up under these trees on the pine needle bed where it will be warmer," said Brent.

The flag was large enough to cover the entire group with enough to tuck around the two guys on the ends, Griffin and Cable. The group listened to the trees whispering to each other.

"You know, if I close my eyes it is just like we are back camping with Mr. Alpin and Ms. Mitre. The trees sound the same here," said Mia as the canyon got darker. Stars began to appear and indicated the outline of the trees. The lights of a plane sailed high overhead.

CHAPTER 27 — WHATEVER IT TAKES

There are different ways to do innovation. You can plant a lot of seeds, not be committed to any particular one of them, but just see what grows. And this really isn't how we've approached this. We go mission-first, then focus on the pieces we need and go deep on them and be committed to them. - Mark Zuckerberg

Long before sunrise, the breeze grew to a pulsing wind. The group was protected under their weathered DreamLand flag, but the whispering of the trees changed to a loud growl. Most of the group were awake but pretended to be asleep, either to not bother the others or in denial of their current situation. The ground was not as comfortable as it seemed when they were tired after the long day. Griffin got up as the sky just began to lighten. He poured a bit of kerosene into the old vegetable can and set Cable's modified pot on top and measured 2 scoops of water into it. He struck a match and lit the fuel vapor into a yellow flame and then held the match, cupped in his hands.

"You might be warmer with shoes on," whispered Cable.

"Ya, maybe," replied Griffin as he blew out the match and the two of them extended their hands to shroud the makeshift stove.

"Are you starting the rice?" asked Cable.

"Yep, I couldn't sleep anyway. I figure the earlier we start, the more daylight and cool weather we have."

"I don't think we have to worry about getting hot with this breeze," said Cable. "At least it is blowing our direction, but that might change as the sun comes up. What are you thinking we will carry the rice in?"

Griffin picked up an empty Mattoni water bottle and used his knife to cut it all the way around, about 4 cm from the top. He then pushed the top section over the bottom section like a cap and presented it to Cable. The water was just beginning to bubble so he dumped one scoop of rice into the water.

"I will be glad to have something besides rice to eat, but so thankful we found this," said Cable.

The glow in the sky was starting to reflect on the river. Their eyes followed the sparkling ribbon to where it met the landslide. They both sat, silently, pondering their situation and the unavoidable solution. Something moved at the tarp and they noticed Maggie's eyes were peering out. Cable looked into the pot and then back at Maggie and then held up 5 fingers. She closed her eyes and tucked under the cover for 5 more minutes of warmth.

She heard the spoon stirring in the pot and the clank on the rim and knew it was time to eat. Silently she slipped out from under the cover and into the dim chill of the morning.

"Good morning," she said. "Are you making our breakfast and take-away order?"

"Yep, Griff made our travel container," Cable said as he handed the modified bottle to Maggie, stirred the rice, and blew out the flame under the pot. He offered a spoon to Maggie and held the pot for her to scoop out her first bite. He followed and then offered the pot to Griffin who took a bite as he was putting on his socks and shoes. They continued passing around the pot and filling the travel bottle until they had enough. They should probably have eaten more but they were burdened with the weight of the day.

"How much water do you think we should bring?" asked Maggie.

"We should bring at least 2 bottles each," answered Cable.

"That's what I was thinking too. At this point, we could just drink from the stream. We are either getting out of here soon or we won't have to worry about water," said Griffin.

Cable topped off 6 bottles from the large drum. "Anything else, besides our jackets and flashlight, that we should bring?" he asked.

"I think that's it, fast and light today," said Griffin. "All set?"

The rays of sunlight had not reached their camp yet but were crawling down the mountain slope above the road. Brent had his eyes open and stuck his hand out into the cold and gave a thumbs up and whispered good luck.

The three returned the gesture and turned down the road. They stretched as they walked toward the landslide and then picked their way through the jumble of dirt, plants, and boulders. It was apparent that only limited foot traffic had traversed this obstacle since the slide. The road once again appeared on the other side of the slide and looked much the same as they had driven. All three picked up their pace to a jog, most of the time side by side.

There wasn't much to talk about, and they were focused on their mission for the day, doing whatever it takes to get out and get help. Before long, the sun reached the canyon bottom and the road, but the air was still cool and moist and smelled fresh with a hint of pine.

They continued their pace for a couple of hours before they took their first break at an especially picturesque location where the road was elevated above the river at a sharp left turn that offered a view out into a valley below them.

"Is that," pointed Cable. "Is that smoke rising out there?"

"I think so. That means there are people," replied Maggie.

"I get 1 bar of service on my phone, but it won't send a text. Just spinning," said Cable.

"Do you see the straight lines of trees where it meets the farmland?" asked Griffin.

"How far is that?" asked Maggie.

"I figure still another couple hours run," said Cable. "It looks like the distance down Sycamore Canyon to the ocean where we trained for cross country."

They ate some cold rice and drank about half their first bottles of water. Next to the guardrail where they sat were 4 empty beer cans, new and brightly colored.

"I think we are getting closer, maybe people coming up on motorcycles or something. Let's go," said Griffin.

They continued to run over another hour as the canyon opened to more of a valley, the road becoming straighter and with fewer weeds but more trash.

"Never thought I would be excited to see trash," joked Cable.

"There's a sign," observed Maggie.

"Leaving DreamLand," read Cable.

"Yes, that's what we are trying to do," said Griffin.

"I hear cars," said Maggie.

"There's a highway, not many cars, but that is a highway," said Cable as he pointed.

As they climbed over a slight rise, they could see a highway and a heavy gate that blocked access to their road. A large sign stood next to the heavy gate, but it was covered over in cheap, warped plywood. The outline of the sign matched the colors and decoration that was on their banner. As they reached the highway, they could see a sign marking the distance to the nearest town, Útočiště 2 km.

"Should we keep running or catch a ride?" asked Griffin.

"If a ride should present itself, I would not decline," said Cable. "This matches the direction to the glow we saw in the sky, so I think we are heading for both the village and the city."

As they ran, they heard cars coming from behind, so they turned around and waved but the cars hurried past. Again, they heard cars and turned and waved, but this time an old sedan pulled to the side of the road just ahead of them. They kept running and came up to the passenger window where a young girl sat next to a gray-haired man who was driving. She cranked her window down.

"Do you speak English?" asked Maggie.

"Yes, a biet," smiled the girl.

"We are the group who crashed in the plane a couple weeks ago," said Maggie slowly and clearly. "Have you heard about the plane?"

"Ano," she said as her eyes widened and smiled.

"No?" asked Cable.

"Sorry, yes, yes. Ano is yes," she said. "We see on the tv. You are dead."

"There are nine of us and very alive!" exclaimed Griffin.

"Nine of you?" she asked.

"Yes, but the others are still on the road to DreamLand," said Maggie, but the girl looked confused.

"Do you know DreamLand? The roller coasters? The lake?" prompted Cable.

"Lake," said the girl blankly.

"Yes, the lake and the amusement park, DreamLand," said Maggie.

Suddenly the older man leaned over, "DreamLand?"

"Yes," said Maggie.

The girl and the gray-haired man conversed quickly in something they did not understand. Not even one word was recognizable except "DreamLand." Then the girl asked, "You crashed at DreamLand?"

"Yes," confirmed Maggie.

The girl and man continued talking and pointing in the direction of the road by which they ran. The man shook his head.

"That is very far and on the other side of a lake, says my grandfather," said the girl.

"Yes," said Cable as he motioned to the road and then made an arc over the mountains, and then motioned as if he were swimming and finally pointed. The girl and man looked at each other and then talked. The grandfather asked them a question in Czech.

"He asks, where are others," said the girl.

"Up the road on the other side of the," Maggie paused, trying to find a simple word for 'landslide'. She motioned with her arms showing sliding and tumbling as she said, "mountain."

The girl turned to her grandfather and explained but seemed unsure of the end. The grandfather asked more questions.

The girl continued, "There is a place the road stops at the river."

"Yes, that is where our friends are," confirmed Cable.

The girl nodded to her grandfather whose eyes widened. He motioned for them to get in.

"My name is Maggie."

"I am Eliška (*Eleashka*) and my grandfather is Pavel."

"Where are you going?" asked Griffin.

"We live in Útočiště (*Utahcheaske*)," said Eliška.

"I think that is the town we saw on the sign," whispered Maggie to the Cable and Griffin.

"We can take you other places," said Eliška.

"We need someone who can drive past the gate and to the river and carry 8 people," said Maggie.

Eliška and Pavel talked and then he said something and smiled and said, "Jan (*Yon*)."

A few minutes later, Pavel turned up a dirt road that wound its way up through farm fields to a large barn. There were odd vehicles parked outside, tractors, 4x4s, and things they had never seen before. Animals were wandering around the barn and a huge man in overalls came out of the barn carrying a shotgun. Maggie tapped Cable and pointed at the man.

Pavel pulled the car up next to the man as he rolled his window down. The man lowered his gun and smiled. The two talked and Pavel pointed to the back seat and up into the mountains.

"Jan runs a 4x4 tour company and knows the roads," said Eliška as she opened the car door and invited the three to meet Jan.

Jan smiled and walked to the barn. He lifted the large wood beam and swung the door open. Inside loomed a huge military green, flat-nosed truck.

Griffin drooled, "What is that?"

"Tatra 813, monstrum," boomed Jan as he climbed up into the cab. It let out a thunderous belch of black smoke and roared out of the barn as he parked it on the grass. Griffin pulled out his phone, turned it on and snapped a photo.

"That will work," said Griffin.

"Made in Czechia," said Jan in a thick accent. "Get your friends now?"

"Yes, yes," said Maggie. "Road to DreamLand."

"Anooo. Anooo. Eliška?" said Jan.

Eliška looked at her grandfather and he smiled and nodded, and she turned and pointed to the passenger doors of the Tatra 813. They climbed the step and opened the doors, Griffin in the front seat next to Jan. The monster cleared its throat, bucked and lurched out of the yard. Instead of going back to the highway, he steered left down a narrow path between two fields, the huge tires crushing the grass on either side of the path. As it reached the end of the field, it did not slow, but merely swerved to miss some trees and dove down an embankment into a wide arroyo that was covered in rock and sand. Ahead of them was a river, much the same as the one that their van was parked next to. Jan sat up straight, as if to see better, and turned slightly right. "Sit. No. Hold on," he advised as the behemoth plowed into the river with a wave of water jetting upward from either side. The beast bounced over rocks, vomited a cloud of black smoke,  and made a deafening growl and hiss as it pulled itself up the bank of the river and up a slope on the far side.

The angle was so great that they could not see what was ahead until the front end crashed down onto the level pavement and they were looking at the road that they had jogged down just a couple hours before. Jan looked over at Griffin and Maggie on the right side and smiled.

"OK?" he asked as he bellowed a mighty laugh.

"Ano," replied Cable, trying out his first word in Czech.

Jan smiled and laughed as he drove his mighty tour van.

"Just think if we had this instead of the UAZ?" said Griffin.

"UAZ? Made in Russia. This is Český, like me," smiled Jan as he maneuvered up the road. He did not bother to avoid brush, branches, or even any rocks, that were smaller than a toaster. About 25 minutes later they reached the edge of the landslide.

Jan asked Eliška some questions and then she asked Griffin, "How much further? Jan is worried that he will tip over on this slope and the river is deeper here in the canyon."

"Blow the horn. They are right there," said Griffin as he pointed a few hundred meters up the road. Jan understood enough and suddenly an air horn blasted through the canyon. Cody, Mia, Abby appeared right away, running, and waving their arms. Tears ran down Maggie's cheeks and Cable wiped his eyes.

Maggie whispered, "We made it. We are all safe."

Jan replied with two more blasts of the horn and then shut down the beast.

Everyone piled out of the Tatra and ran to meet the others on the other side of the slide.

"What do we need to bring?" asked Griffin.

"It looks like you brought plenty, Griff," said Abby as she hugged him. "Just our bags and the 2 Pelicans, I think."

"And the flag," said Mia. "Let's hang it in the engineering lab."

They grabbed their bags and helped each other across the slide. Jan easily lifted 5 of the group into the bed of the truck with the luggage and loaded 4 into the cab with Eliška.

"Ready?" he laughed and fired up the V-12 diesel engine and blasted the horn one more time to punctuate his deft maneuver to back the truck up the slope and turn around while hanging the front wheel off the edge over the river.

"I go easier on the way back," he said as he gestured to the back of the truck. Each big bump was celebrated by a yell and laugh from the back.

About 35 minutes later they had reached the slope that drops to the river. Jan paused and there was some discussion in the cab.

"Sit against the front wall of the truck," yelled Griffin out the window, followed by a thump, thump against the metal wall. The beast crawled over the edge of the mountain and down, into the river. He went slower this time, but the truck still lurched over hidden boulders and then bounced its way up the far bank of the arroyo. He followed the same path back through the farm, but the farmhouse and yard were filled with people when they returned. Seeing the people, he pierced the air with 2 shots from the horn and laughed.

As they pulled into the middle of the crowd of people, Griffin could make out several types of uniforms and official cars. In the hour and a half since Pavel started making calls, there was enough time for the local police from Prague, emergency rescue personnel, and the media to show up. Nothing this exciting has happened in Útočiště in many months, so locals arrived to see the "dead" students from America.

A man and woman, dressed in dark uniforms, exited a white car with blue and bright yellow markings and the word POLICIE on the door and approached the group as they were climbing down from their perches in the vehicle.

Addressing Sterling, apparently because she looked the oldest, "I am Officer Svoboda of Policie České Republiky. Where have you been?"

The group closed ranks in front of the two officers. Griffin replied, "Our plane crashed at the DreamLand amusement park and we—"

"DreamLand?" Officer Svoboda cut him off. "That is far and there is a lake and no boat."

"Yes," replied Cable, as he smiled. "We made a raft and crossed the lake."

Sterling continued, "The crew was killed, and these kids saved us."

"They saved you?" scoffed the officer. "They are just kids."

The media crew had been mingling and asking questions but heard the conversation and started recording video.

She replied, "Yes, all the crew and the other adults on the flight were in the front of the plane and perished, but these 8 students figured out everything. I would not have lived more than a couple of days."

"We wouldn't have lived, either, if you didn't figure out how to make rice interesting and help us have time," said Shelbi.

"What have you been eating for the last two weeks," asked the reporter.

"We found rice and some cans of food in the warehouse," replied Shelbi.

"Is this being shown in America? We need to tell our parents we are OK. Did you really think we were dead?" asked Brent.

The police officer tried to bring the conversation back into his control and replied, "Yes, the airline reported that they lost contact but the last data they had was dropping elevation near the German border. They have been looking east of here and figured that the plane went into a lake in Germany."

"We almost did, but landed on the shore in front of DreamLand," said Griffin.

Many members of the community nodded and smiled at the mention of DreamLand.

"But there is no boat or way across the lake after the big storm sank the ferry and washed out the road," said the female officer. "How did you get across the lake?"

"They made a raft and put a van on it," exclaimed Sterling.

"A van?" asked the reporter.

"Let's start from the beginning," said Maggie. "But first, we need to call our parents. Is there cell phone service here?"

"Yes, there should be," replied the officer.

The students were already turning on their phones. Phones were beeping with notifications. Cable was one of the first to be done.

"I texted that I am alive and will get back to them soon. I texted Mr. Alpin too. Let's start from the beginning." The students took turns telling the whole story, meanwhile taking time to make and answer calls from parents. The crowd of locals was growing, and another media car pulled up as the shadows stretched across the grass.

Pavel and Eliška waved and started to retreat from the crowd, but Griffin could see them over the heads and yelled, "Eleeeeshka. Pavel. Thank you so much." The students circled the pair and hugged them.

Maggie's phone rang again. She looked and said to the others, "Bekah. Bekah Milano from school."

She clicked her phone, "Hello?" After a short pause, "Yes, we are alive and in a village outside of Prague…. Really? Yes, that would be amazing. Tomorrow? OK, thanks and talk to you then."

"Bekah has just arrived to film on location with her dad in Germany and is coming to get us tomorrow about 10 a.m. and take us back to Munich for easier flights back home. She sounded really concerned and wanted to help."

"Ya, my parents were all starting to think that we were dead because we had been missing so long," said Mia.

"Mine want to fly here tonight. I will text them that we are headed for Germany in the morning," said Maggie.

The reporters and locals continued to ask questions as the long shadows became evening. Jan had been absent from the group but reappeared, his voice booming through the crowd.

"Now you stay with me tonight. I have BnB on the hill. Dinner is ready. You all go home now," he said as he waved his hands at the crowd and laughed.

"Dinner. I forgot how hungry I am. Yes, please," said Griffin.

The group, including Sterling, followed Jan up the hill to a large house with many lights on inside.

"This is Karolina, my wife," said Jan as they started up the stairs.

The group entered the dining room and stared at the bowls and baskets of food, bread, meat, fruit, and fresh vegetables. Maggie and Shelbi both wept.

"We have been so focused on getting out and we are here, safe, having dinner. I can't believe it," sniffed Maggie. "It is all catching up."

Shelbi stood up with her crutch and moved to Maggie and put her arms around her and wept. "We are OK. We made it."

The group gathered around Maggie and held each other in silence.

Cody spoke softly, "Dear Heavenly Father, we thank you for keeping us safe. Thank you for these friends and thank you for our new friends here. Thank you for this food. Help us to never take anything for granted. Amen."

"Amen," said Jan and Karolina. "We eat."

"Yes," the group said in chorus and collapsed into the chairs. Each person held each bowl, looked, and smelled and thoughtfully served each item.

"This is the best food I have ever had, and I don't even recognize all of it," said Cable as the group laughed and cried together.

They finished dinner with wonderful conversation, the conversation that one looks back at and is amazed that it was done in broken English, complete with hand motions and pantomimes.

"We have beds for all of you," said Karolina. "Come."

She directed them in pairs to each room in the great farmhouse, even a couple rooms on the ground floor for Shelbi, Sterling, and

Brent. "There are robes on each bed. Just leave your clothes in the hall and they will be clean by morning."

The beds were like pillows with down covers. No one could remember falling asleep. Cable even forgot to change out of his clothes, just leaned back and was asleep before Griffin came back from taking a shower.

CHAPTER 28 — LEAVING

I love those who can smile in trouble, who can gather strength from distress, and grow brave by reflection. 'Tis the business of little minds to shrink, but they whose heart is firm, and whose conscience approves their conduct, will pursue their principles unto death. - Leonardo da Vinci

The sunlight was streaming in, bright and warm, by the time that Maggie and Mia first stirred. They smelled fresh, baked breakfast, they started knocking on doors to get everyone up. They found neat piles of clean clothes in front of each door and retrieved theirs on their way back into their room. The students showered and gradually made their way downstairs and found a basket of fresh rolls, sausages, jams, eggs, and various spreads with juice and coffee. They served themselves and sat around the dining room and out on the porch. Despite the time difference, they were on their phones, assuring families that they were OK and headed to the airport soon. Maggie walked out into the garden and took a photo of the farmhouse.

Jan entered the dining room, "Your ride will be here soon. Ready?"

"Yes, we will make sure everyone is ready," said Maggie as she and Mia ran upstairs to get everyone.

"I have booked a flight from Prague too," said Sterling. "Can I catch a ride with you?"

"Sure, we travel light," joked Cable. "Here comes a shuttle. Jan, no more Tatra?"

"No, they won't let me on the streets. I only drive in country. My friend, Tomas, runs airport shuttle in the city. Wants to drive the dead Americans," Jan laughed.

Everyone filed out of the farmhouse with Karolina holding a basket, "For your day," she said. "You need it, too skinny." She pinched Griffin.

The group loaded into the shiny shuttle. Jan gave Maggie a big hug. "Have a good flight."

"Thanks for everything. It was the best night's sleep, great food, and the amazing Tatra," said Maggie.

Jan laughed, stepped up into the shuttle and waved to the group.

The shuttle bumped down the dirt lane and headed through the village of Útočiště and on toward Prague. The houses, farms, and roads sailed by the windows, all quite surreal to be back around people, electronics, and the concept of time. Maggie opened the basket and found it was full of the fresh baked items. She bent over the basket and inhaled each delicious scent.

The shuttle driver did not speak much English, but he was friendly. "Terminal 2 or private?" he asked.

Maggie replied, "1 for Terminal 2 and 8 of us for private."

"Terminal 2 first. Many TV cameras there, too," he said with a smile.

Shelbi and Brent looked at Sterling, realizing their eminent farewell. Shelbi was sitting next to Sterling, so she reached her arm around her. "You are going to be OK. You have a new start."

"I have a new start and a new perspective," said Sterling. "Thank you all for taking care of me. I," she paused and wiped a tear. "I used to make cut-throat business transactions and value stuff and how I look. You solved problems and looked past emotions and outward image to get to what mattered and it saved our lives. Thank you."

"We're engineers. We're good at ignoring emotions," said Cable.

Sterling smiled, knowing that Cable cared deeply, enough to lighten a sad moment. The shuttle slowed in front of terminal 2, but there wasn't much room to pull up to the curb with all the media cars and reporters. Tomas smiled and stopped right in front of the cameras. Sterling stood up and the group of students circled her in one hug. Cameras flashed outside.

Sterling stepped toward the exit, "Thank you. Love you all." She stepped outside into the waiting crowd. The shuttle door closed, and Tomas slowly moved the shuttle away from the crowd. The reporters were distracted with the arrival of Sterling as the bus slipped away. It moved along to terminal 3, where no one was waiting, except one woman with flowing black hair.

"That's Bekah," said Maggie.

The shuttle stopped and Bekah jumped on board as the door was just opening. "I'm so glad you guys are OK. I can't believe what I saw on the news. You engineered your way out of a plane crash in the mountains?! I want to hear how you calculated the buoyancy required to move a van across a lake."

"You nerd," joked Cable. "Thanks for coming to get us. We will give you the inside story. And yes, we scienced the snot out of the situation, just like Dr. Watney did in *The Martian*. We missed you. Next time you will have to join us on our trip."

"Speaking of trip, the plane is ready," she said. "By the way, my dad was talking with Mr. Alpin and the school and they have your flight all set to leave out of Munich early this afternoon and you will be in LA by tonight. Follow me. We exit down these stairs."

"I just got the email with the tickets," said Maggie.

As they started across the tarmac, Griffin saw the plane and exclaimed, "That is less than half the size of the plane we came in on, but maybe that is a good thing."

The group walked up the small, flip-down stairs. Cable helped Shelbi up the stairs.

"Wow, this is your normal life?" asked Shelbi.

"So, my dad is in the middle of a movie in Germany and he wanted me to come do some scenes for a few days," said Bekah. "The news all over America is that your plane went down in some weather and they thought it crashed into a lake so they couldn't find it. It did not have the transponders like the big planes, so they have been flying search patterns near the German border."

Cody replied, "The plane did drop elevation back a ways but stayed in the air until we had a sudden drop and landing at DreamLand, an abandoned amusement park."

"Then I heard the news reports last night at our hotel in Germany and wanted to help. So, how did you get across the lake? Everyone is wondering, and I think you built a raft or boat like the discussion we had in class."

"Yep, made a raft out of log ride logs," said Griffin. "The tough part was making it strong enough to support a van and then make a propulsion system to get across the lake."

"Then Mia had the idea to make a sail," added Cable.

The conversation continued for a while, repeating many of the details of the experience, but with greater passion for the engineering details. The group snacked on the fresh bakery items. Eventually, Mia, Cody, Shelbi, and Griffin fell asleep. Maggie closed her eyes and leaned on Cable. Abby and Brent were looking out the windows for the entire flight. Just before touchdown, Maggie and Bekah woke everyone, but as the wheels touched down it shook them into a painful memory.

"That is still going to take some time getting used to," said Cable.

Bekah said, "We will be landing on the east side of the airport for the private planes and then take a shuttle around the airport and have to enter the regular terminal and security. I will take you there and then head back to our film location."

The group gathered their small bags from the plane and the shuttle was parked next to the plane. As the shuttle pulled into the departures area of the main airport, there were no media vans or reporters.

Bekah said, "This is another advantage of not flying commercial, no one knows what flight you are on, so we should get you right to the ticketing area for your flight home without being bothered. No promises when you land in LA. I want to hear more details about how you engineered the cooking, water, and the van. I meant to ask about the van. OK, I'll see you back at school in a couple of days."

"Bye. Thanks again," everyone joined in and hugged Bekah.

They slipped right into the ticketing area and Maggie had the email with all the flight information, so she went first.

"We don't have much paperwork," began Maggie. "We are the kids from the plane crash," she whispered to the ticketing agent.

"Oh, my. All of you here? OK, yes. Let me see your booking number."

Maggie presented her phone for the number.

"Just a moment. Let me see what I can do," she said. "Do you have any bags to check?"

"No, the plane crash reduced our baggage count a bit," joked Cable.

"So sorry, yes. OK, I have changed your seats for the return. You are not all together but I fit all 8 of you in business class. I am printing your boarding passes now." Each person received their pass and the group moved through security and stopped for food.

"I still have my VISA card and want to grab my Toblerone bars," said Shelbi. "We ended up eating the others as emergency rations and I really want to just savor some nice dark chocolate."

They enjoyed some blended coffee drinks, sent and received more texts and calls from home and boarded their plane, a new A380. In-flight movies, food, and beverages kept the group quite comfortable and rested. A few fell asleep as the wheels left the ground.

CHAPTER 29 – HOME AGAIN

The ache for home lives in all of us, the safe place where we can go as we are and not be questioned. - Maya Angelou

The flight was the most comfortable, and restless, that any of the group had ever taken. Every bounce and shutter of the plane caused each one to look out the window or watch a flight attendant to judge the mood of the staff. Everyone breathed a quiet sigh when the wheels touched down in LA. The group walked up the sloped corridor of the international arrivals. All the parents were lined up to receive the group, reporters had cameras ready while checking their phones and makeup. Mr. Alpin and Ms. Mitre were standing at the edge of the group.

The students wept and hugged their families while cameras flashed and video rolled.

Mr. Alpin said, "I am so proud of you. I can't wait to hear about all your engineering. I saw news clips and heard about you making a raft and water jet with a van. What incredible innovators you are. I also have something for you. Here is a copy of the complete conference report with all the papers and yours is in there. Even though you weren't there to present, and I was distracted with all the news and reports of the likely plane crash, your paper was included in the report and there was a lot of interest in what you wrote."

Reporters were asking questions and pressing in on the group. For some, the idea alone of surviving in a remote place with nothing but your training and brain to keep you alive would cause sweat ooze from one's skin. For most of these kids, that is just part of solving the world's problems, but getting surrounded by strangers in a crowded place is the worst feeling of all.

"Let's get out of here," said Shelbi as she raised her crutch and pointed the way through the crowd.

The group moved toward the door, and they looked at each other. Their eyes seemed to say everything at once. They had survived together, struggled together, and did everything that had to be done together. They moved to each other for one last hug.

"I forgot to turn off the water line at the tank before we left," said Cable.

"Goodbye, Cable. See you back at school," said Brent.

"I have totally lost track of time," said Griffin. "When are finals? What day is it?"

"It is Tuesday and next week is finals week," said Maggie.

They left the airport and went home. In some ways, it was familiar to be back home, but at the same time, it was different. They had changed. They had become innovators and survivors.

As they entered a room and lights illuminated at the flick of a switch and water poured from the faucet, they appreciated every drop. The full refrigerator amazed them with choices. The clock on the wall was even different. It was still a number, but the day would be measured differently from now on.

Maggie was home, sitting in her living room, tired, but excited. Her sense of time had been warped by the 9-hour time difference and long flight. She thought about looking at the time on her phone but realized it didn't matter. She realized she was tired, hungry, and school was the next day.

"I understand the painting by Dali of the melted clocks in a whole new way," said Maggie. "I had never thought of it before. The clocks are all outside in nature, so no wonder they are distorted and useless. The construct of time is irrelevant in nature. We woke up, worked, and slept by the daylight and not by what time it said on a phone and we worked to survive. Let's eat dinner, but no rice, OK?"

xvii

After dinner, Maggie's mom asked, "Are you going to school tomorrow?"

"Of course, finals are next week. And I miss my friends."

"We are so relieved to have you home. Sleep well and see you in the morning."

Griffin sat in his family room with his family gathered around. He was telling stories non-stop. Griffin's family was used to his crazy stories, but these seemed so far-fetched. They listened but looked at each other in amazement and disbelief.

Mia wasn't satisfied to just take notes or read other's stories to escape the world around her, or in her past. She was part of a team, a winning team. At home, she told her story of being a survivor and an innovator. Her parents couldn't believe her wild tales, but they also couldn't deny that she was changed. She went back to her room and found a blank journal and turned to the first page and wrote.

Scarred, but not defeated.

NEXT, my life begins today. I am strong. I am not defined by my past or my failures. I turn a new page each day and will become the person I want to be. I am... Her mind drifted to memories of strapping bedframes to fiberglass logs and sailing across a lake with a van and then continued, *I am amazing! My broken parts don't matter, and I can make something new from them.* Mia drifted off to sleep with the pen still in her hand. Her last thought was that it didn't matter who believed her stories. She knew who she was now, and no one could take that from her.

Cable sat at the dinner table with his younger siblings, telling tales of floating a van on logs and driving in a Czech military vehicle. They asked when they could go see the Ferris wheel and fun rides too. His mom was racing around placing plates of food on the table, wiping faces, cleaning spills, and nodding as Cable filled the room with enthusiastic stories. Cable resumed his normal routine of filling sippy cups, clearing dishes, and getting his siblings ready for bedtime. He tucked them in as they asked for more bedtime stories of DreamLand. At last, he sat down on his own bed, ran his hand across his soft pillow and never remembers falling asleep.

Abby woke with a start. The quiet darkness enveloped her. Was it all a dream? She felt the sheets and it was home.

Her mind raced to think of details and connect if it was real or if it was DreamLand.

Her thoughts were still stretched thin and twisted, so she reached for her phone to check the time. She tried to think. Time. Her dream was so vivid. They talked about time. Oh, was it real? Should she pinch herself? Does that even work? If only there were some evidence.

Her right hand banged the nightstand in the dark. "Owe! My hand! Oh, my hand."

ABOUT THE AUTHOR

Greg Gillis-Smith started working for NASA when he was a sophomore in high school. He graduated in Engineering from Cal Poly San Luis Obispo and continued working as a mechanisms engineer for JPL/NASA, on missions that went to Mars, Saturn, comets, and Earth-orbit.

Moving out of aerospace, Greg became an engineering director for Capstone Microturbine where he worked with customers and contractors to understand how to install the unique generators. This experience outside with architects and contractors led to a world of working in the construction and redevelopment industry, where he also ran his own company for over 10 years as a project manager and engineering consultant.

Greg had always wanted to find a way to share his experience and background by teaching engineering and had a passion to teach at the high school level to motivate and educate new engineers. This opportunity came out of the blue after speaking at a local high school. Many of the characters and conversations in this book were inspired by actual classroom experiences. He loves teaching, but he also sees a way to impact youth beyond the classroom by writing adventures that teach and inspire.

WWW.GILLIS-SMITHAUTHOR.COM

LINKS AND CREDITS

i   en.wikipedia.org/wiki/Pi

ii   en.wikipedia.org/wiki/Steinmetz_solid

iii   en.wikipedia.org/wiki/E_(mathematical_constant)

iv   en.wikipedia.org/wiki/Natural_logarithm

v   viewbook.calpoly.edu/academics/college-of-engineering

vi   www.rexnord.com/blog/articles/what-is-l10-life

vii Paweł "pbm" Szubert / Wikipedia, licencja: cc-by-sa-3.0

viii Erik Zeterberg, cc-by-sa-2.0

ix   Jorge Franganillo, cc-by-sa-2.0

x   Druschba 4, cc-by-sa-3.0

xi   Mdkoch84, cc-by-sa-2.0

xii Zoltan, www.theoverlander.org/ovl-forum/27/354.html

xiii kepzadventures.com

xiv abandondedexplorers.com

xv   Jano Gallo, cc-by-sa-2.5

xvi Public Domain 1/31/2014

xvii Mike Steele, cc-by-sa-2.0